FOREVER YOURS

HELEN OVBIAGELE

Contents

Chapter 1

The car stopped and the driver got out smartly to open the door for Halima Kadizu. She murmured her thanks, flashed him one of her smiles which never failed to send him briefly into the land of fantasy, and stepped out elegantly. She was no raving beauty, but was strikingly attractive — and she knew it for it had taken years of practice under keen maternal supervision to acquire it. Twenty-two, medium light skinned, tall and well groomed, long permed hair drawn sleekly back, stance studied, and movement unhurried, she oozed charm and good breeding. There were just four in her family — father, mother, her brother Haliru and Halima herself. The Kadizus had decided that two children were about all they could afford to

love and look after comfortably and had turned
a deaf ear to the families who had condemned
their action as selfish. A woman who had no
problem with childbearing should keep having
babies until the supply gave out, parents on both
sides had argued.

When they were younger, Haliru and
Halima had envied children who had lots of
brothers and sisters to play and fight with. Later
they realised the advantages of a small family
— more attention from parents and life was not
too much of a struggle. They were not spoiled
by their loving parents and only reasonable
demands were met. Haliru, who had studied
Agriculture at the University of Ife, had joined
the federal civil service and was working in
Vom in Plateau State. Their father was still in
service, but their mother had retired and now
kept a poultry farm on the Kaduna/Zaria Road
where they had a lovely bungalow in vast

grounds.

When Halima left the University of Ibadan, where she had studied French and Spanish, she had been offered an appointment by the Ministry of External Affairs as a trainee translator. She loved languages and, apart from Hausa, her maternal tongue, she could speak the other two major languages fairly well. She looked forward eagerly to the day when she would be one of the top translators in the country. Life would be perfect. Meeting Bala Sumiyar had changed all that. It happened when she had just completed her national youth service in Jos and she was spending a week with Haliru who was the general manager of the dairy farm in Danso, a village on the outskirts of Vom. She had intended to spend another week in Kaduna with her parents and then it would be off to Lagos and her job. She was excited.

Towards the end of her one week stay, Sule, Haliru's assistant, who was an executive member of the Nigerian Archaeological Society, invited her to the Society's annual dinner/dance, which was taking place in Vom. She was asked to be one of the hostesses and she went in the company of Haliru and Laraba, his fiancée.

The party was well attended and she was kept busy showing the important guests to their seats and seeing that they were served by the waiters. Later, she was asked to be one of the judges at the highlight of the evening, the Miss Relics Beauty Contest. She felt tired and her stomach rumbled with hunger as she took her seat. There had been no time to have a drink or a bite since the evening began and no one had thought it necessary to offer her anything. She looked enviously at Haliru and Laraba as they tucked into their food on the other side of the dance floor. She caught her brother's eye, rolled hers and pointed discreetly to her stomach. He grinned at her and gave her the thumbs up sign. She made a face at him.

There were ten contestants in all and there was a heated discussion among the judges as three of the girls were tied in first position. They were pretty indeed and it was really difficult to decide who should have the crown. At last the chief judge said this would be done by ballot. Halima was relieved when it was all over, and, after the winner was declared, and the chairman for the occasion had claimed her for a dance, she sneaked out for some fresh air in the garden where some customers were being served drinks and sandwiches. The sight revived her hunger pangs and she looked into her purse for money. Now that most of the people at the party had had their food, she was too self conscious to go and help herself at the buffet table which was in a conspicuous position. People might think she was a greedy hog going for a second helping!

She would tell Haliru and Sule off afterwards for not looking after her, she fumed. After all, she was supposed to be a guest and she should have been entertained. Luckily she had some money with her. She hoped it would be enough for a sandwich and a soft drink. She went to the bar at the far end of the lawn and gave her order. Oh, no, madam, said a deep voice behind her. After all the hard work you did this evening, you deserve more than a sandwich. And why come out here to pay for your food when there's an array of delicious dishes in the hall?

She turned round to look into the smiling face of a tall, dark, attractive man in flowing white robes and a high embroidered cap. She recognised him as one of the guests at the high table. Another hostess had led him to his seat and she had not caught his name when the master of ceremony had introduced him, but she remembered thinking how cool and dignified he looked as he took his bow. He looked thirtyish, but could be less as those flowing agbadas usually added years to their wearers. Studying him more closely now, he did not look so handsome as noble in bearing. He had broad shoulders and looked strong and athletic. He's probably a fine horseman, she concluded.

Oh, hello, she greeted, smiling at him. I thought the food inside must be cold by now, so I came out here for some chicken sandwiches. Are they hot, these sandwiches? he asked in a wondering tone as he looked at the bread the grinning man behind the counter was slicing. Oh, er, I don't think so, but . .. She seemed embarrassed. Look, you're going to have proper food and I'll get it for you. You stay here.

Thank you. She smiled at him gratefully. The sandwiches did not look appetising. Would you like any special dish? Rice, eba, tuwo, moimoi or dodo and beans? Or would you prefer a mixture of light food for the weight conscious lady? He winked at her. Some salad and moimoi would do, please. Okay, I'll be back in a moment. The name is Bala Sumiyar.

Halima Kadizu.

He nodded. I had made some inquiries before joining you out here. You're Haliru's sister. You're acquainted? Only slightly. We run into each other once in a while either socially or in the course of business. Soon he was back with two plates of food. To keep you company, he explained as he picked up a fork. Thanks, she murmured as she began to eat.

He began to tell her about himself. He was the group general coordinator of his family business concern — SUMIYAR & SONS LTD. Their head office was in Kaduna where he was based, and they had a tannery in Bauchi, a canning factory in Kano and a textile mill in Kaduna. His main duty was supplying these factories with raw materials and equipment. This involved some travelling, but mostly in the northern parts of the country. He was the fifth of a family of seventeen children; about nine of them were involved in the family business. Actually, the idea was that all or most of the children would eventually join the business in one capacity or the other, according to their profession. Already they had a doctor, a lawyer, a food analyst, a plumber, a carpenter, a nurse and a secretary. He was the odd jobs man, he claimed, having done business administration.

Danso, where he had a country house on a very small cattle ranch, was his favourite place to which he retired now and again. It's my favourite place too, said Halima. It's so picturesque. Everything is so simple and the villagers are so friendly. What do you want to do with your life? asked Bala. Halima told him a bit about herself and her future plans. As she talked, he listened thoughtfully, gazing deep into her eyes, a strange expression on his face. She found this a bit disconcerting and she stumbled over her words. This embarrassed her even more as she was usually cool and confident in the company of men. Not that there had been many or that there was anyone special, but it had been part of her upbringing to appear as cool and collected as she could in public. It makes you stand out and look something anywhere, her mother had said.

It makes you look cold and arrogant and it drives away hot blooded and exciting men, Rahila, her close friend and confidante had told her. She laughed then. Rahila was such a rebel.

As she looked at Bala, Halima wondered what Rahila would think of him. She was bound to approve of him. Not that it mattered if she did not. Their tastes in boyfriends differed but this did not affect their friendship. Bala's penetrating gaze disturbed her. She sensed instinctively that he would be able to exercise over her the sort of power that no man as yet had ever done. He could have her eating, out of the hollow of his hand. And she was so strong willed! He had neither said nor done anything to make her come to this conclusion but she could sense it. Already there was this pull between them. It was electrifying and it made her heart pound. It was frightening too, as if it was something over which she had no control. This is ridiculous, she told herself. AH she had to do was to get up and walk away from him! But she knew she could not, would not.

Halima, he said softly, putting down his

fork. She looked at him. He looked serious now, the boyish grin had vanished. You've a strange effect on me. I can't define it. Your presence fills me with a glow of excitement. Nobody had ever inspired such a feeling in me. I wonder what's happening… His voice trailed off, and he looked puzzled. He was obviously not used to telling a lady what he felt about her. Bala was not timid and he loved the company of women but they did not form the focal point of his existence. His money and looks ensured that he got those he wanted, and he never took them seriously. Halima, however, evoked something exhilarating and heady in him and this made him fiercely possessive even on such short acquaintance. He wanted to own her, take her away, love her and keep her locked up for himself only. It was crazy!

Let's dance, he suggested, getting up and adjusting his robes. She hesitated, glancing furtively at his left hand. He noticed. Oh, ah, he stammered, sitting down again, you're wondering if I'm married. Well, I am, and I have two daughters aged nine and six. But I've been living apart from my family for almost a year now. He had never had to explain his marital status to any lady and he felt slightly silly doing so. He hoped Halima was not one of those ladies who were anti-married men. She was. She did not like relationships with married men whether they were separated, divorced or widowed. She sat looking at Bala, silently cursing this unknown wife; a thousand questions racing through her mind. Had they been close? Did he love her? Whose fault was it that the marriage had not worked? It couldn"t have been his! Such a gorgeous man! She felt acutely jealous that another woman had ever been closely related to him — had lived with him; loved him; borne his children!

She was puzzled at her train of thoughts. Why, the man was a total stranger! What was happening to her? Does it matter that I'm married, or was married? he asked, searching her face anxiously, trying to read her thoughts. He was furious with himself for his anxiety. Many women would jump at the chance to make his acquaintance and there he was almost pleading to be acceptable to her. He felt his ego taking a beating and yet he could not walk away from her.

It shouldn't you know, he continued earnestly. Take it that I'm free as far as matrimony is concerned. I mean, I lead my own life and consider myself free. Suddenly Halima felt an uplift in her mood — excitement at what tonight's meeting might lead to. She still did not want to dance with him, though. It might break the magic. She just wanted to go to bed with this happy feeling and conjure up lovely dreams. So, with a promise to call to see her at Haliru's the next day, he left.

She settled into the back seat of Haliru's car and gave herself up to the blissful thoughts of Bala. The next few days were going to be fantastic! Already, her romantic mind was at work. She could picture both of them strolling down lonely country lanes, arms around each other, stopping every now and again to hug, kiss and whisper sweet nothings, basking in the warmth of their love and happiness. There was no doubt that they had fallen in love. Oh joy!

When Halima told her brother the next morning at breakfast that she had met Bala Sumiyar and that he would call to see her later in the day, he pursed his lips. What's the matter? she asked. Don't you like him? He told me you're slightly acquainted. True. We bump into each other occasionally and say hi. Out with it, bro, she said, slightly irritated. Brother

and sister were quite close and she wanted
Haliru to like Bala. What don't you like about
him? He's okay as far as businessmen go —
two thirds honest, passably sociable, fairly kind
and helpful.

However, I find him aloof and arrogant.
He must be about my own age but he behaves
as if he was ancient. You know what I mean; he
wouldn't let his hair down and behave like one
of the boys. Well, if that's all you've got against
him, he can't be too bad, eh? If you say so. He
behaves like one of the nobility, with his nose
in the air. Say, you aren't sweet on him already,
are you sis?

Between you and me and that doorpost,
she whispered, it's more than that actually. I
may even be in love with him already. Heavens!
he said in an awed voice. Fast work I must say
for someone like you who does not wear her
heart on her sleeve. What magic did the man

use? She laughed. There's magic between us all right. I feel as if I've known him for a long time. The usual lover's line, he said, half to himself through a mouthful of bread and egg. I'm not for or against Bala, but isn't there a wife somewhere? Yes, in Kaduna. He told me they've been living apart for almost a year. I thought you were allergic to married men in whatever shape or form.

That's right, but in this case an exception could be considered. Aha! Bending the rules for him, are you? The blighter must have something to offer after all. Although what it is, is all lost on me. If I were a lady I wouldn't smile in his direction let alone fall in love with him. Thank goodness you're not a lady. I wouldn't want competition from you. Still, watch it, sis, and be as sensible as usual. Okay, thanks. I'll be off to work now, he said getting up. What do you intend to do all day?

Nothing in particular. I know. You're going to sit around dreaming about Bala. He ducked as she aimed a piece of bread at him. By the time Bala turned up in the afternoon, she had become sulky and sullen while waiting. He had not specified when he would call, but she had thought that he would be so anxious to see her that he would be there early. He found her in the front garden trying to concentrate on a book.

Hello, he said, jumping down from a Land Rover. She caught her breath as she stared at him. The transformation was delightful. He looked extremely boyish in an embroidered jumper and tight fitting slacks which emphasised the slimness of his waist. Gone was the dignified look of the businessman. In its place was this dashing young man ready for adventure. Her heart thumped painfully as he sat down near her and picked up the book she was reading. Hi! She greeted me weakly. Did you have a pleasant day? Fairly. I would have come earlier but I went to bed very late and woke up only a couple of hours ago. Did you miss me? he asked in a soft voice. I missed you. If you've been sleeping and have only just got up, how could you have missed me? To share my sleep with me, and also be with me since I got up, he said smugly. She looked away, her thoughts in a whirl. Why are you frowning? he asked, pulling his chair forward.

Am I?

A minute ago, yes. Have you had lunch? I haven't had anything yet today. I brought a basket. I thought we could go for a picnic. There's a nice spot I know where… She got up.

The picnic is a good idea, but I don't think I want to go to this nice spot you know. Why not? he asked in surprise. I'm sure I won't like it. I think it would be more fun if we discovered a spot together. I don't want somewhere you've taken other girls to. She bit her lips and stopped. Oh, was all he could find to say as they stood staring at each other, fascinated. I'll go and change, she said, breaking the spell.

She returned to find him pacing the garden, lost in thought. She was wearing a sleeveless, light green catsuit in adire material, large hoop earrings, a green headband and flat sandals. She looked seductively attractive and his eyes lit up in approval. She blushed, glowing inwardly. I brought along some cheese, fresh milk and fruit. That's fine, he said. I hope I'll be able to eat. I thought you said you've had nothing yet today. You're right but now you've taken my appetite away. That is, my appetite for food. His eyes ran hungrily over her. My goodness, I must watch it, she said to herself. I'm totally lost to this stranger, and that's not a good thing. I should apply the brakes and I can't control myself. He smiled at her with satisfaction as if reading her thoughts and concurring.

Come on, let's go, he said, taking the basket from her. Which direction do we head for? he asked when they got to the gate. Left, please. He looked at her with mock severity. Get this straight, my dear girl. I'm not going to any picnic spot some other guy had taken you to. So, what do we do? She laughed happily. We'll discover a spot together. It's the only fair thing to do, he agreed. Let's toss for direction.

They found a beautiful spot at the foot of a small hill. The area was alive with wildflowers of varying colours. They sniffed contentedly at the heavy mixture of perfume in the air. Adding to the beauty of the place where the butterflies flitting from flower to flower and the birds hopping about in the long grass. They could hear the moos of the cows and the occasional shouts of the cattle hands in a nearby pasture.

They decided to explore the area first, so they locked up the vehicle and set off, hand in hand. It was a long walk which took them to the other side of the hill. On their way back they stopped at a stream, rolled up their slacks and took off their shoes. They sat on a large stone by the edge and put their feet in the water to cool, feeling very much at ease in each other's company. Halima, he said after a while, do you feel the same way I do, that we've been acquainted for a long time? She nodded.

What do you think of me? Can't say yet, she said cautiously. Give me some time. Oh, look, she cried out excitedly, pointing at the water. Tiddlers! I've always wanted to catch some with my bare hands. She got up and waded into the stream. Careful, he warned, getting up too. Don't go too far out. The stream might be deeper than you think. He was too late. She was sinking. Her arms flailed helplessly in the air as she tried to regain her balance. In a flash he went after her. He had to stop and pull back quickly when one of his feet gave way. It would be foolish to allow both of them to sink.

He appraised the situation. Halima was stuck in the mud up to her knees and there seemed no danger of her sinking further; at least not for the time being. He got a long stick and tried to pull her out. The more he pulled the further she sank so he had to stop. She was staring fixedly in front of her, paralysed with fear. He fought down his own panic as he thought of a way out. He cursed himself. He should have remembered how treacherous these seemingly shallow streams could be.

He should not have stopped with Halima at the stream. What made the situation worse was that streams were usually deserted in the mid afternoon as the men were in the fields, the children at home and the women still in the market. He would have to go for help. After some consoling words to Halima, he hurried off in the direction of the village. When he got back with four men, thirty minutes later, panting and anxious, he found her sitting some distance away from the stream, with about six women fussing over her, cleaning her up.

Apparently, as soon as he had left, the women, who had been on their way back from selling fresh milk and butter in the market, had called at the stream to wash their calabashes and fetch water. When they saw Halima they wasted no time at all, knowing exactly what to do. They had rolled some big stones from the water's edge to where she was stuck, climbed on to them, and with stout sticks had dug around her and had pulled her out. Weeping with relief she hugged and kissed them all until they were as covered with mud as she was. Bala thanked them profusely but when he offered them some money they refused shyly, murmuring that they had been glad to help.

They moved to another part of the stream and were soon busy washing their calabashes and chatting. He helped Halima to her feet and examined her legs. Apart from a few scratches, she was fine. Precious, he began in an emotional voice, if anything had happened to you, I would never have forgiven myself. I should not have brought you this way. Forget it, Bala, she said. The poor man looked so strained. It was not your fault in any way. We discovered the picnic spot together, remember. Picnic! he exclaimed. I'd forgotten all about that. Come on, let's get on with it. Race you to the car.

They tried, but could not run as they were

both limping slightly from cramp. The afternoon was still young and beautiful and by the time they laid out their picnic things and began to eat they had almost forgotten about the incident, as they became once more absorbed in each other. He insisted on feeding her. She bit self consciously into the pieces he offered her and blushed when he ate what was left and drank from her cup.

He went about it solemnly as if it was some kind of ritual. When she shook her head to indicate that she was full, he also stopped eating too. He wiped her mouth tenderly with paper serviette and they cleared up together. She dozed while they listened to the five o'clock news on the small transistor radio he had brought along. Here, Halima, put down your head and go to sleep, he told her, indicating his lap. She rubbed her eyes and blinked. I'm not sleepy at all, a bit tired perhaps but.

You go to sleep, he said firmly. She acquiesced and lay down, using his lap as a pillow. She shut her eyes. Shall I sing you a Hausa lullaby? She smiled sleepily and he brushed her forehead with his lips. Part payment for my services, he explained, smoothing down her hair, and beginning to sing in a low husky voice.

She woke up with a start and shivered. She had slept for almost an hour. It was getting dark and the air had become chilly. Everywhere was calm; even the insects and the birds that were preparing to settle down for the night went about it in a hushed manner. In the distance, she could see the movements and hear the low mooing of the cattle as they were being led home. The cattle hands swung their sticks and shouted as they went along.

Bala, of course, had fallen asleep. His mouth was slightly open. She felt like shutting it with her lips. She didn't. Instead she got up and began to carry their things back to the Land Rover. He woke and jumped to his feet looking round wildly for her. She hid behind the tree. Halima, he called anxiously, where are you? Here, right behind you, she laughed.

He turned and pulled her into his arms, kissing her fiercely on the lips. Her arms went around his neck as she surrendered herself to his kisses. They pulled apart only to go into each other's arms once again. I had a frightening dream back there, he told her on their way home. What was it about? We were both walking along this lonely road, arm in arm, when you suddenly broke into a run. I gave chase but you ran faster, sobbing loudly and I never managed to catch up with you until I woke up. I don't like it. I'm worried. Why? she laughed. It was only a dream. Yes, but why would you want to run away from someone who's as crazy about you as I am? I probably thought you were the devil or something, she said lightly. You don't take dreams seriously, do you? Generally, no. This one, yes, since it's about you. You've captured my heart in a way no other lady has ever done.He frowned. Say, Halima, you aren't thinking of leaving me are you?

Leaving you? she echoed in surprise. How can I leave you when there's nothing yet between us? Is that what you think? Surely you must feel something. There's no doubt I've fallen in love with you. I don't need a lifetime to know that. I like you, Bala, and I've enjoyed being in your company. He looked at her and smiled. That's something to build on. He was quite sure that in no time she would fall helplessly in love with him. Without any conceit, he was going to work at it using all his charms. He could feel something smouldering between them which would be difficult to put out. He had this crazy desire to possess her and take total charge of her. Not even Muni, his wife, of whom he was fond, had succeeded in arousing that sentiment in him.

He and Muni had grown up in the same neighbourhood and had attended the same Arabic School as children. Theirs had been a platonic relationship but the families had pounced on the opportunity to arrange their marriage. They had liked the idea too as they got on quite well together and the thought of not being in love had not crossed their minds, at the time. Even when it did, they were determined not to make an issue of it and they worked hard to make their marriage work. It didn't.

As she grew older Muni realised that she wanted a husband who was warm and demonstrative in their relationship and she was profoundly disappointed when Bala"s attitude became more cold and distant. She was quite fond of him and she tried as hard as she could to show him this by being warm, attentive and affectionate with him. It all had no effect whatsoever on him. She was baffled. Had something brought this on or had he always been like that and she had not noticed?

Before their marriage and early in the marriage he had been full of good humour and he had treated her with great respect and kindness. Later, their relationship had become that of a lord and his subject. It was as if he was afraid that by treating her in a comradely manner he was lowering his prestige. She found this attitude silly in a man as enlightened as he was, even though they both came from a background where the husband ruled the home as if it was a little kingdom.

But in many cases, the man did this to show those around that he was a master. In private, he showed his true self, whether affectionate, kind and humorous, or exactly the opposite. Whatever the case, a wife got to know her man. It had not been the case with Bala who carried his hauteur even to the bedroom, behaving during their intimate moments as if he was doing her a favour. She had thought that the arrival of the children would stir something in him. It did. He fell in love with them and could not see or do enough for them. She loved them too, but his attitude made her feel excluded in his affection and it hurt a great deal.

Discussing how she felt with him had not improved matters as he had failed or refused to see her point. To him their marriage was perfect and their relationship satisfactory. They liked each other, did not quarrel much and had lovely children.

Above all, he kept the family in luxury. What more could a woman want? Many women would give. anything to change places with her, he had told her. She saw no reason why he should treat her in such a condescending manner and she refused to resign herself to such a marriage when she was still only in her twenties.

Perhaps if she took a job and proved capable of fending for herself he would see her in another light and their relationship would improve, she thought. Her job as the director of the local council's Children's Home. was hectic but most satisfying. She loved children and being able to improve the lot of the unfortunate ones was something she had always longed to do.

Her husband had frowned at her taking up a job, but decided not to interfere since it obviously made her happy. Actually, he preferred not to talk about it and their relationship deteriorated further as she would rush back from work all eager to discuss the day's events only to be met with a cold rebuff. He would not discuss his job either. Resentment crept into the home and there were bouts of cool silences followed by polite communication. Some months of these and they both agreed on a trial separation. Six months after he moved out of the house, they both admitted that they were happier not living together. Divorce would follow later. Bala continued to support his family financially and could see and take the children out whenever he liked. The children accepted the change without much fuss since Mummy was around as much as possible and Daddy phoned to chat almost every night.

Muni was satisfied with the way things had been settled. She missed her husband but would rather be alone than have him around with his cold indifference. It hurt her pride that he was unable to love her; still she felt no jealousy when she saw him with other women after they had parted. She sometimes felt sorry for some of the starry eyed girls who fell for him. How frustrating it must be for them as the affairs never lasted more than a few weeks at a time. No woman could ever warm that cold heart of his, she told herself. What a pity! Such a charming man. She was glad she had her job.

Bala was aware that his marriage had not been as successful as he would have wished it but he refused to accept any responsibility for its failure. He felt he had amply fulfilled his role as a husband and a father. To him, it was Muni who had broken up the home, moaning about love and companionship.

Halima needed no persuasion to stay the extra week that Bala needed to wind up his business in Vom for that tour. They were so much in love and spent so much time together that parting each evening became unbearable.

She would see him off to his car and they would cling together; he would see her back to the door only for her to see him to his car again. Heavens, is that how you both carry on? Haliru exclaimed one night when his sister finally came in. How? she asked in a faraway voice. I mean the. clinging and the shuttling forwards and backwards like two drunken fish. You were watching us, she accused him. You should be ashamed of yourself. Of course I was watching you, and I'm not ashamed of myself. You're my kid sister and I've every right to watch whatever you're doing. My, what a performance! I'm glad Laraba is not like that. It would make me sick. Tell me, sis, do you do that each time he's leaving?

Yes, and it's going to get worse now that I know we've a spectator. I'm so happy I feel like singing. Go ahead. It's nice to observe people in love. Shall I bring out my guitar and accompany you? No, thank you. Tralala. All right. Hm! Do you two find time to eat and drink like the rest of us ordinary people? Of course.

He eyed her. You look a bit thin to me. Mum will say that I've been starving you. Goodness knows that there's no shortage of food in the house of a conscientious farmer, and I've done my best to put everything at your disposal and urge you to eat. Don't worry. I'll soon be off your hands. Bala and I will leave tomorrow evening for Kaduna. How long are you staying there? Just a few days. I've to take up my appointment on Monday. Looking forward to it? In a way, yes, although not as eagerly as before. Bala hates Lagos but he said he'll come down there every month to see me. Not right away, I hope.

Right away, of course, she laughed. Don't you need time to settle down and get to grips with the job before having distractions, no matter how pleasant? Bala's no distraction and we cannot bear to be apart for long if we can help it. The distance is not that much by air. Yes, but won't the job suffer if he's going to be around that frequently? I'll see it doesn't. I want to make him like Lagos so much that he'll pack his bag and come to live there. His company has a branch there. But you don't like Lagos.

I don't, but that's going to be my base for a while yet, so he has to be there too.

Hmm, and you'll both live happily ever after. Perfect! You still don't like him. I put up with him, don't I? I allow him to wear out my driveway with his presence. Surely that's enough. It isn't. You don't expect me to love him too, do you? You can have a try. I wonder how Mum and Dad will react to him? I've done your dirty work for you. I've informed them that our beloved Halima has fallen for an unworthy fellow called Bala Sumiyar, and that they should not be surprised to see his offensive person at odd hours as he seems incapable of breathing without you.Thanks, that was thoughtful of you.

I mentioned the 'married' bit too so that it won't Be a shock to Mum that her daughter's principles have been adulterated. Thanks again. That will save me from doing a lot of explaining. Oh, anything for peace in the family. Halima's parents were not enthusiastic about the relationship but they had no grounds for objecting to it. Not that they would have wanted to as they believed in leaving their children as adults to make their own decisions. This had brought them all close in the family and there were hardly any secrets amongst them. Bala found himself a bit in awe of this couple who treated him with so much courtesy that he was always ill at ease in their presence.

A day before Halima was due to leave for

Lagos, he persuaded her to extend her stay by two weeks so he could accompany her there. She wrote off to the Ministry feigning ill health. Her parents watched anxiously but quietly as she and Bala became almost inseparable. Rahila did not mince her words on the rare occasion she was able to get her on her own. She liked Bala but was highly critical of the way he was possessive about Halima.

At this rate, you'll lose all your friends, she told Halima. He monopolises too much of your time. The relationship is too stifling to be a healthy one. Halima admitted that she sometimes felt hemmed in. It was as if he was trying to isolate her from everybody. He grumbled if she wanted to call on friends or stay at home with her parents. He took her on business visits and enjoyed introducing her to his friends, but frowned if he felt that she was giving too much of her attention to any of them.

If she went shopping or to her hairdresser's his driver would take her there and hover around the door. She found this flattering sometimes, attributing it to his great love for her.

Love nothing, scoffed her friend. He's a nice guy but you ought to assert yourself. If you don't do so now, if and when you get married he would want to trample you under his foot and you wouldn't like that, and the quarrels would begin. Halima silently agreed with Rahila as she herself had thought along those lines, but only when she was away from him. When they were together, his slightest touch, his grave caressing eyes were enough to melt any resistance she was going to put up. The only sensible thing that resulted from the situation was her resolve not to get married yet. She reasoned that if being in love made her that weak willed, surely she was not mature enough emotionally to take the serious step of getting married.

During her last weekend there, he took her to Funtua to meet his parents and see the places where he had spent his childhood. It was an enjoyable but exhausting visit and on the way back they chatted for a while, then suddenly a heavy silence hung in the air. It had to do with her departure for Lagos.

She could not keep on postponing it indefinitely. In those days of high graduate unemployment the position would be offered to someone else. Already she was feeling guilty about the extra two weeks she had taken. A few kilometres from Rigachuku Railway Station, he stopped the car under a mango tree. He got down and walked quickly towards a line of beggars that was heading for the car. He got out his purse, distributed some coins and the people retraced their steps shouting their thanks and praying loudly. That's that. Now they'll leave us in peace, he said as he got back and settled into his seat. Are we staying here for a while? she asked, looking around. The sun was going down and the area was fairly busy with men and women making their way home from the farms. He was silent. She repeated her question. He turned his face away, and when he turned back there were tears in his eyes as he took her in his arms, burying his face in her luxurious hair. She felt weak and embarrassed. She had never seen a grown man cry before except in films.

What is it darling? she asked as she felt his tears on her neck. She pulled away to look at him, a slight panic rising in her. What was the matter? Was he going to tell her that he suffered from some incurable disease? Only something connected with death would bring tears to a man's eyes. Heavens, let it be something she could bear. He meant so much to her. He pulled her back into his arms. Don't leave me, Halima, he said in a quiet voice. Don't go away to Lagos. I've tried to put up with the thought of our separation, but I can't.

Is that why you've been looking so dejected this afternoon? she asked, relief flooding her. Yes. Don't go. Not seeing you frequently, touching you, kissing you and making love to you would slowly kill me. You'll be hundreds of kilometres away living a life I"m no part of. I had not wanted to have to make you change your mind, hoping that you would not want to go away from me. But we had agreed that you'll come down to Lagos every month so that we can be together. True, but what sort of a relationship is that? We'll grow further and further apart until we'll have to force thoughts of each other. I don't think that will happen. Don't you trust my love for you to withstand the test of distance between us?

I do, but that does not eliminate the temptations that will abound. Temptations abound here too even if I were to stay. I"m not worried about leaving you here although I"ll miss you terribly. So, you're refusing to consider staying, is that it, my love? The tears were back in his eyes again. Halima's heart melted and the fight that was rising in her began to subside. Oh, how she loved him! But this was blackmail! The rosy and interesting future she was looking forward to was gradually fading away. For she knew she was losing the battle. In fact she had already lost it. She was going to stay although she had not said so yet. She felt frightened and angry at the realisation that Bala could manipulate her the way he did. Would their relationship always be like that? She, ready to acquiesce to anything? She made one last effort.

We both have our jobs. We'd be so busy

that we wouldn't notice the days fly past. Absence makes the heart grow fonder. I will notice the days. They'll stretch endlessly before me and I wouldn't be able to concentrate on anything. I'll end up a nervous wreck. You won't Bala, and you know it. Then you don't realise how deeply in love I am with you. He shook his head sadly. Her heart went taut.

What do you suggest we do? she asked quietly, arguing within herself that a career was not everything and that she too would be incapable of concentration if she left him behind. His eyes were shining when he realised that she was yielding, but he tried not to look triumphant as he took her in his arms. We'll find something here for you to do, darling. Something quite interesting. You'll see.

Yes, but what exactly? She pulled away from him, somewhat annoyed with herself that she had given in without much struggle. This is a dead town as far as my line of profession is concerned. You can't really say until you've tried, he said as he started the car. There are lots of jobs around and somewhere there must be one that you would find suitable. Come on, let's go home. You must be tired and hungry. It's been a long day. He moved a short distance and stopped. Now what? she asked impatiently.

He gave her his grave and solemn look which enhanced his handsomeness, and made her heart do a somersault. Her anger ebbed. I recognise and appreciate the sacrifice you've made for our love, Halima. You've shown me that you are really very fond of me, and I will never forget this unselfish gesture. If it were possible to love you more than I do at the moment, I would. You've made me proud and shown me what true love is. Thank you. She leaned back, tender tears springing to her eyes, her whole being suffused with happiness and love. She did not feel she was making any sacrifice, she had merely followed the dictates of her heart.

The news that she was no longer going to take up her appointment in Lagos did not go down too well with her parents. They were glad that she was no longer going to live far away, but were not happy that her relationship with Bala was important enough to her at that stage to make her give up a career she had carefully planned and was looking forward to.

Sometimes Halima thought wistfully of what her life as a translator might have been, particularly when she read of visits to the country by foreign dignitaries. She was sure she would have worked very hard to earn being given duties on those occasions. What a wardrobe she would have had, and how exhilarating it would have been out there in the forefront sharing the limelight with all the important people. Still, she found her job as assistant office manager at the British Council enjoyable and satisfying. Her duties involved dealing with people, a thing she liked; staff matters including staff welfare, conditions of service, recruitment, maintenance of Council properties, etc. It was a hectic and challenging job and she felt utilised to the full.

Chapter 2

Four months later, she moved into a small bungalow that Bala got for her in Abakpa. Living with her parents had been lovely but it was nothing compared with the satisfaction of having a place of her own. She and Bala spent many happy hours shopping for what to put into it, arguing amicably over the prices. He wanted to get the costliest of whatever was required, but she preferred those moderately priced. I know you're paying, darling, and I think it's terribly generous of you, she told him, but the most expensive things are not necessarily the best or the most practical. I think I"ll settle for this set of furniture.

She had to put down her foot on the question of domestic help as well. He wanted to flood the place with four guards, three gardeners, a cook, two maids, two stewards and about three or four hangers on whose duties even he could not define. Just like at his place!

In true Moslem fashion he felt he should provide for those less fortunate than himself, and if anyone showed any inclination to work, he employed him first and thought of what duties to give him later. But for the vigilance and iron rule of Hajia Asabe, his housekeeper, Halima was quite sure his house would be crawling with people of doubtful character. Asabe was a tough, middle aged widow who hated indolence and fired on the spot those she felt were not giving their best service. Bala did not always see eye to eye with her, but he liked and trusted her and knew that she ran the place efficiently. I'll feel invaded with so many people around, Halima protested. They'll be working.

Doing what precisely? There'll be too many for a small place like this. I think I"ll have a gardener, a maid, a steward and two guards. I'll do my own cooking. But I don't want you to lift a finger. After a day in the office you"ll need to put up your feet. Thanks darling, but cooking and a little bit of housework will help me unwind. I can't understand you," he grumbled. You're different from most women I know. You've refused to live with me until my divorce is through and we can get married, and you won't allow me to provide as much comfort for you as I would like to. But what you've done, Bala, is sufficient. You've spent so much money on me that I feel guilty. I work, you know, and I can provide many of these things. I want to do more because I love you. I'm afraid of you finding someone else.

Thanks, but you ought to have noticed that

material things do not mean very much to me. I don't judge our love by what sum of money you're able to spend on me. If you had nothing I would still have fallen in love with you. He said nothing but gave her a look which showed he did not believe her. That look revealed to her something she had never given much thought. Bala, she said coldly, you don't think I fell in love with you because of your money, do you? She moved away from the dining table at which they had been sitting and went to look out into the garden.

It was overgrown with weeds because the gardener had not begun work yet. It was the rainy season and the flowers were in bloom so the sight that greeted her was a mixture of dazzling colours.

She and Bala had planned how they would transform the place into a veritable Garden of Eden, but how she stared with unseeing eyes.

How could he harbour such mean thoughts about her? Put her in the category of graball women? Did others see their relationship in that light too? He went and gently turned her away from the window. I'm sorry, darling, he said, tracing an outline between her ear and her neck with his lips and finally kissing her gently on the lips. Maybe I'm too much in love with you. If you really loved me you would trust me. I'm jealous too in my relationship with you, but I try to be sensible and not think that you're having an affair with all the women who call at your office. If we were living together things would be much easier.

They'd be worse because I'd refuse to be put under lock and key as I'm sure you'd want to do. He laughed because that was what he would feel like doing. Hell! He had not realised that being in love with a woman would ever arouse such a jealous feeling in him. He would have to go easy if he did not want to lose Halima. But what about Alhaji Kato and Malam Sani? The latter was her boss in the office and, although he was aware of a cold war between the two, his shrewd mind told him that that could veil a budding love affair.

Alhaji Kato was a business acquaintance of his and also Halima's landlord and neighbour. He had five wives, was wealthy and a notorious womaniser. He always dropped in for a chat whenever Bala was around and he did not conceal his admiration for Halima. His greedy eyes would roam all over her and no amount of subtle hints or downright rudeness from Bala would make him realise that his company was unwelcome. Instead he would teasingly ask Bala how he came to deserve such a fabulous lady.

She found it all flattering and amusing at first; even flirting with him when Bala was there. She had to stop when he began to call on her when his friend was not around. When Bala heard of this he wanted to get her another house but she loved the place so much that he did not have the heart to insist on her moving. Halima had this feeling of sitting on dynamite and she knew that a showdown with Malam Sani, her boss, was inevitable. It was only a question of time.

When she was new and green on the job, the relationship between them had been cordial enough. He had not taken her seriously, referring to her as my dollybird assistant. He was in his late fifties; a devoted family man who had retired from the State civil service to join the British Council as Office Manager. He was painstakingly hardworking and efficient and felt capable of putting in at least eight more years of service before going on final retirement.

He treated Halima like a favourite daughter, giving her light and unimportant duties, preferring to do the bulk of the work himself and deal directly with the staff under her supervision. Thus she was bypassed by her subordinates and for the first few months she had very little to do. She felt edged out and useless, and the thought of not really earning her salary plagued her conscience. Her mild protests to her boss had no effect as he told her in a jovial manner that she should be glad she had nothing to do, and that she could spend the time painting her nails and looking even more beautiful. She was not to be deterred and, on the advice of her father, she marched into Malam Sani's office one morning armed with a copy of the list of duties she had got along with her letter of appointment. He shrugged as he tossed the paper back to her.

It's all right there on paper, but can you

really perform those duties? I would not have been employed, sir, if I were not thought fit to perform them.

Hmm!

The man was insufferable! Did he think I came in through the back door? she asked herself as she recalled the tough interview which had led to her being appointed.

You must agree, sir, that you've given me no opportunity to carry out these duties as you deal directly with the staff under me and leave me out in the cold. How will you be able to assess my performance when I have not had the opportunity of carrying out my duties?

Oh, oh, I begin to understand, he laughed. The bit of fluff really wanted to work! To him a woman's place should be in the house performing the duties assigned to her by nature. You want a good report on the performance of your duties? You want to shine at your job, eh? Ha! Ha! Have your eye on promotion later, don't you eh? he added sarcastically. She was not to be put off. Everyone likes to get on, sir.

Hmm! he said thoughtfully. He would have to tread carefully now that the girl was not content to sit back and fold her arms. He'd probably have to allow her a place in the running of the department. Apart from being his assistant, she was on good terms with the director of Centre and she might make her grievances known to him.

What would happen if you went on leave or fell ill, sir? How could I deputise for you effectively if I have had no practice at running the place; getting the staff used to taking instructions from me? she was asking.

That was it! Go on the leave he had been postponing and let her make a mess of things.

He would egg on one or two members of staff to make things difficult for her. She would show herself up woefully and, mercifully, by the time he came back, she would have earned herself the sack for incompetence. He would be able to convince the director that the old way was better; having the supervisors report directly to him. A deputy was not really necessary. It was most disappointing when he got back from holiday to discover that things had gone smoothly in his absence.

He refused to believe it when his old faithful in the department reported that Halima had handled the job well. When, a few days after resuming duties he was told jokingly in the corridor that his absence this time had not been too obvious because things had gone the way he would have wanted, he became perturbed and it was then the hostility actually began. He was cunning about it. In public he was known to be very friendly and protective towards his assistant, and everyone thought she was lucky to have such a nice boss. Alone with her, he gave her hell, criticizing her every move, thereby hoping to destroy her self confidence and make her perform badly.

However, she carried on diligently with her duties and hoped that the situation would change, although she was gradually becoming frustrated and unhappy. Things went on like this for eleven more months, then one afternoon, the situation got out of hand and it was all over. Halima had gone to Malam Sani's office to report on a particularly difficult assignment he had given her and which she had carried out the way he had directed. She had just had lunch with Bala, who as usual was very attentive and loving, so she was bubbling with happiness and confidence when she went in. She was sure she would at last earn a word of praise from her boss for a job well done. She was completely deflated when after giving him an account of the assignment he told her in a cold voice that she had behaved in her usual stupid fashion.

She controlled her rising temper to ask politely what she had done wrong. Nothing, he replied, except that you're trying all the time to prove that you're a "Miss Know-it-all"". You think because you've been to the University you know everything. Experience and maturity counts a lot in this job you know, in spite of paper qualification being the norm these days. We old hands cannot be easily written off like that. We've a lot to offer. You think too highly of yourself. You try to impress everyone with what you regard as high efficiency. Nonsense! Pure nonsense! Pushing yourself forward! Trying to get noticed. Thinking you can replace me!

Halima's eyes flew wide open with astonishment as she realised that the man was actually jealous of her ability to carry out her job properly. She stopped pleading with him and became decidedly calm. A mocking smile played on her lips as she stared at him. The worm was feeling insecure about his position and wanted to use his hostility to edge her out of her job. No way, sir!

I'll go along to my office now, sir, she said, getting up. She threw him a disdainful look, held herself very straight and prepared to march out of his office.

The girl's mocking smile provoked him to anger and he knew that his last remark must have brought it on. Already he regretted making her aware of his insecurity as it was likely to make her despise him. So, to hurt her, he remarked with a cold sneer as she was about to leave the room. Just a minute, Miss Kadizu.

She swung round. Yes, Malam Sani? she asked politely. Eh, I believe you're quite an intelligent lady who could perform very well in this department, that is, if you"d address yourself more to your work instead of chasing after rich married businessmen. She gasped, unable to believe her ears. You gave Sumiyar no rest until you broke up his home and deprived his family of a husband and a father. Your victory will only be short-lived, however, as he's fond of his wife and will go back to her. You're crazy, Malam Sani, she shrieked, beside herself with rage. I'll take you to court for this. You"ve pushed me too far. You can't take me anywhere. You've no witnesses. No one will ever believe your story. I'm no fool, my dear."

It was true. No one would believe her. He was too cunning for her. It was at this point that she threw the half glass of Coca-Cola on his desk in his face, ruining his immaculate flowing white robes. She expected him to scream at her, instead there was a satisfied smile on his face as he pressed the button on his internal telephone and summoned his secretary. Halima almost collided with the latter at the door.

The rest was short and simple. Malam Sani went to make a report to Mr Peters, the Director of the Centre. Halima was called in, asked her version of the incident and told to go and apologise to her boss. She refused as she was not convinced that she was guilty. No one would have been able to keep her cool under the circumstances. She was also angry that the Director seemed not to have believed that the amiable Malam Sani was capable of making such a mean statement. Anyway he had already telephoned him pleading with the Director to be lenient with his assistant and saying he wished he had not reported the incident. If she did not want to go and apologise to her boss, then she would have to be suspended from her duties. She resigned from her job.

Bala applauded her action and told her that she had done him proud by not apologising to a lowdown dog like Malam Sani who would have gone about boasting that, but for his grace, Bala Sumiyar's girl would have been kicked out of her much needed job. He told her she did not need to work and he offered to increase her allowance. Now that his divorce was through, he went on, why did they not get married and make things easier? Did she not love him? She assured him she did, but did not feel ready for marriage yet.

She sometimes asked herself why she was reluctant to take that crucial step in their relationship when she loved him so much. Was she afraid of total commitment to him? Was she afraid that they would cease to love each other when they became man and wife? She was sensible enough to know that no woman can remain a bride forever. Yet it was as if she was waiting for something to happen. Something to push her forward to the next stage of her life; whatever that stage might be.

I've not really done much with my life since I left the University, have I? she asked Rahila as the latter was putting finishing touches to the dress she had designed. In what way? Well, the only remarkable tiling I've done was to fall in love with Bala, and now that I don't seem to be capable of holding down a job, he has become the axle of my day-to-day existence. What would you have done in my place?

I would not have thrown away the job at the British Council. Certainly not at a time when you were beginning to enjoy it. Yes, but could you have put up with Malam Sani's two faced behaviour? I would have controlled my temper and played the same game with him too. That is, be nice and sweet to him in public and be really nasty to him when we were alone. I thought of that too but decided that with a fox like him you can never be too careful. He might have a hidden tape recorder to record a particularly provocative scene, or might switch on the intercom so that his secretary could follow all that was being said.

Hmm, that's true. Perhaps it was best to quit. It's better to be one's own boss. Yes; but how possible is that? Not everyone can be as lucky as you've been, running a hotel and a garment factory almost single handedly. I've had fairly trustworthy assistants and I work very hard. I work hard too, and that's why I'll not stay at home as Bala has asked me to. Male chauvinist, murmured Rahila under her breath. Hang it! she cried in disgust. I just can't get these sleeves right. I think I'll call it a day now and go and help put the little ones to bed. I'll come and read them a story. Bala is working late and he'll ring me here when he's ready to leave the office. Does he always know where you are? Yes. His driver is always with me, so I suppose

Hmm, he's too possessive. I think it is a mistake to allow him to manipulate you the way he does. He doesn't. He does, darling. Look at the way you gave up the career you had carefully planned for just because he shed a few false tears. Maybe I didn''t actually want to go to Lagos, Halima said defensively. There are other issues too, I'm sure, on which you've given in to him without a struggle or a thought for yourself. You seem completely overwhelmed by his personality and character. I've watched helplessly as you allowed your will to be gradually crushed by him and all for the sake of love.

Don't misunderstand me, Halima, Rahila said as the other was about to protest. I'm a romantic too and I think being in love is wonderful, but you should love with your head as you get older, and should be able to see things in their right perspective despite your emotion. Right now your life revolves around Bala. When he smiles you're ecstatic, when he frowns you're worried. Also he has to know where you are every minute of the day. In short he's taken control of your life. I know, admitted Halima reluctantly. Although I try occasionally to assert myself and go ahead with what I've decided to do. But to be honest, I do give in most of the time. It's love I suppose. Possibly. The danger is that when he realises that you've become putty in his hand, he might cease to worship you. The excitement and the desire to please would be over once he's certain that you'll sit where you're asked to.

I wouldn't like a situation like that, she said shuddering. What do you suggest I do? Decide what you want out of life. Marriage? A job? Both? An interesting job takes precedence at the moment. Marriage later

Go ahead. Get a job. Where are the jobs in these hard economic times? Have you searched hard enough? No, I'll tell Bala. Aha! Here we go again. Why can't you do things for yourself anymore? You're not the Halima I used to know. The go-getter. It's Bala this, Bala that. It's as if you cannot take charge of yourself. He pays the rent, gives you a monthly allowance, hires and fires the domestic helpers, who are of course paid by him, and he bought all the things in your house. In fact, if you decide to end your relationship with him and not touch anything he's paid for, you'd come out stark naked.

Halima could not help laughing. You should be a novelist, Rahila. You've a vivid way of expressing yourself. Still, what I said is true. Almost. I buy my own clothes. With his money. Look, love, get a grip on yourself. Go All out and get yourself a job without enlisting Bala's help. Discuss your plans with him but don't wait for him to execute them for you. Thanks. I shan't.

There's pride in being capable of providing for your own needs. It would be awful to have to rely on a man for every kobo you spend.

True. Have you met Bala's wife? No, he doesn't like talking about her. I've met the children; delightful girls. You should meet Muni Sumiyar. I wonder why the marriage broke up? He didn't tell me why. Do you know her well? Only slightly.

Pretty?

The phone rang. Rahila picked it up. For

you, she said. Bala. I'll go up to the children. I suppose it's goodnight now, she added. Halima nodded as she reached out for the phone eagerly, eyes shining already in anticipation of Bala's voice. Rahila looked at her friend, shook her head and left the room. She had never seen a human being so consumed, with love for another person. Bala would not hear of Halima going job hunting once again and this led to a row. He became impatient with her.

What are you trying to prove? That you can fend for yourself? If it's any comfort to you I'm acutely aware that you can. Whatever I do for you is just a small token of my love for you. It doesn't mean that I think you"re poor and starving. He softened a bit. It's childish, darling, to keep harping on wanting to earn your living. As it is, people give me funny looks when I tell them that you're looking for a job. Since they regard us as husband and wife they think I must be keeping you short of money if you want to go out to work.

I don't want to be a "kept" woman. What"s your definition of "kept woman"?

A woman who gets every kobo she spends from a man. I want to have a career, prove myself at something. He rolled his eyes skywards, folded his arms across his chest and waited for her to continue, an amused look on his face. Can't you see, Bala, she pleaded, a bit passionately, I can never be the "stay at home" type even when married and with a family. I would want something outside the home to work hard at and be rewarded for. It would make living exciting and challenging. Besides, I would like to earn something on my own whether I need to or not. She stopped, slightly out of breath, and waited for him to speak. He said nothing. Bala darling try and understand, she was going to start pleading again, then she stopped.

Hell, she thought, what am I pleading with him for as if he owns my soul? Does he have to approve every move I make? I'm a person in my own right; free to do what I like with my life. She looked him straight in the eye. Anyway, I've decided to get a job, and that's precisely what I'm going to do. With that she marched away from him, hips swinging provocatively, towards the front door, stopping to pick up her handbag from the couch. I'm going out, she flung at him over her shoulder.

In a few long strides he got to the door before her and barred her way. Where, Halima? he enquired sharply. He looked dangerous. What has come over you? You know it's my exercise hour and I need to concentrate. He used one of the rooms at her place as a study/exercise room, during the week when he could not go polo playing. Go ahead then. I won"t be in your way if I'm out.

Don't be rebellious. You know full well I can't concentrate if you're not around somewhere in the house. This was true. She did not actually feel like going anywhere but she wanted to assert her right to freedom of movement — to show him she could do as she liked. He softened when he noticed the fight in her. If only she knew how lovely she looked when she was angry or pretended she was angry. He led her away from the door towards the settee where they both sat down. He began to kiss her hair, her ears, her eyes, her neck and by the time his mouth found hers, all thoughts of going out, asserting her right to freedom and showing that she was her own boss, had flown out of the window.

Later, he gently but firmly talked her out of picking up a job. He was fed up, he said, with amorous and unreasonable bosses that seemed to lurk wherever she worked. He agreed, however, that she could not sit idly at home and so did not object when she told him of her plans to enrol for gym classes and help charity organisations raise funds. That evening they also fixed their wedding for the following year when she would be twenty six.

She went to bed that night feeling extremely happy and half victorious. She had put her point across, hadn't she? He knew he could not trample all over her, didn't he? Halima received one of the greatest surprises of her life the day she met Muni, Bala's ex-wife. It was purely coincidental. Of all her engagements she enjoyed giving Hausa lessons to the diplomats wives best. This was something she did twice a week.

The classes cut across colour and ethnic barriers and, after the ninety minute lesson which took place in one of the rooms at the

State's Ministry of Information, the group usually got invited for coffee or lunch by one of the members. This gradually developed into a social affair at which topics ranging from motherhood to politics were freely discussed. Halima never missed any of these sessions if she could help it. She would sit in a quiet corner, absorbing the stimulating conversation of these often older and more experienced women.

The women were having coffee one afternoon at the house of Mrs Katinka Abass, the British born wife of a Nigerian diplomat, when a lady called. She was thirtyish or thereabouts, of medium height and light in complexion. Her oval face and pointed nose suggested a Fulani descent and her thick black hair reached to her mid-back. Her sleepy eyes made her seem vulnerable and helpless. Halima could imagine men falling over themselves to protect her from one thing or the other. She herself felt like hugging her and assuring her that she could come forward into the room and that it was not full of monsters. This illusion quickly vanished however as Katinka introduced her round and she chatted with a lot of confidence and self assurance. She seemed to know more than half the ladies in the room, and there was a lot of hugging and kissing. Halima wondered who she was. She had never seen a woman so pretty and exquisite; it left a sweet taste in the mouth. She was simply dressed but in a way that showed off her shapely figure. She had on a sky blue kaftan with a loose silver belt which teasingly emphasised her slim waist. The slits at the sides revealed shapely legs in high silver sandals.

She certainly loves silver, said Halima to herself as she took in the silver hoop earrings, brooch, bracelets and ankle chain. Although lost in her thoughts, she noticed a marked silence in the room as Katinka and her visitor drew near. All eyes were turned in their direction and one or two ladies strained their necks to see better. Halima, a little bit self conscious, looked out of the window behind her to see if there was something going on in the garden which could generate such interest. Nothing. She glanced down at her dress to see if she had coffee stains on it. She had not. What was going on?

The pair were in front of her now and Katinka was nervously making the introductions. Surprisingly, the usually cool Katinka was stumbling over her words. Meet er, er, our teacher, Miss Halima Kadizu. Miss Kadizu, this is my sister-in-law, er, er, Mrs Muni Sumiyar. She's the Director of the Children's Home. Wonderful job she's doing there, she rushed on rather self consciously. Really marvellous job. You could have heard a pin drop in the room. Halima hesitated just the tiniest part of a second before taking the other's outstretched hand and they both smiled as they greeted each other with calculated warmth, eyes appraising each other.

Hmm! Play it cool, Halima told herself as her heart thumped away. So this was Bala's ex-wife! While not actually expecting her to be ugly and nondescript, she had always, on the few occasions she had permitted herself to think about her, pictured a beautiful, but shy and withdrawn lady. She would be the type you felt sorry for because despite her beauty she would always go unnoticed. She had been totally unprepared for this spectacular and confident lady who now stood in front of her, who certainly could not be ignored anywhere. Halima was glad she had dressed well and as usual appeared calm and poised. What could have gone wrong between Muni and Bala? How could any man let go of such a gorgeous and obviously intelligent lady?

Muni looked at Halima with interest. She was not flustered at all, not because she was more mature and older, but because the meeting had not been accidental on her part. Since she had realised that the relationship between Bala and Halima was not that of ships passing in the night, she had been a bit curious, upset and jealous. She had wanted to meet this super girl who had been able to stir up Bala's cold heart and have his undivided attention for so long and who might get married to him. Getting introduced to Halima had steadily become an obsession with her. Friends who would have done it had told her that the idea was silly and totally unnecessary. She had not felt that. If Bala remarried, she had argued, the girls, who were very close to their father, would continue going to his place for weekends and the holidays and it was only natural and fair that she should meet the woman who was going to run the house. Any woman would feel that way. Bala did not want to know, and poor Katinka had almost fainted that day when she had turned up and had insisted on joining the group. She had felt sorry for her embarrassed sister-in-law, but the opportunity had been too good to miss.

She had glimpsed Halima several times from afar but had not wanted to approach her on her own so as to avoid the unpleasantness which could arise from such an encounter. If Bala ever got to know that she had upset his girl in any way, the cordial relationship which existed between them would cease. He had been most understanding and generous up until then and to risk his wrath would have been foolish. She smiled as she shook hands with Halima and complimented her on the success of her Hausa classes, then with a cheery see you around, she and Katinka moved off.

There were a few disappointed sighs in the room as the ladies resumed their conversations. They had anticipated a more lively scene between Bala's ex-wife and his girlfriend. Instead the two ladies had behaved in an outrageously civilised manner — shaking hands, smiling at each other, paying compliments; not even one dirty look or a hiss to brighten the encounter. How very boring!

As she was being driven home, Muni felt a mixture of emotions — with jealousy in the forefront even though she would not admit it. She found immense satisfaction with the new man in her life, yet it hurt to know that another woman had succeeded with Bala where she had failed: She did not need her mirror to tell her that she was more beautiful than Halima. As for background, intelligence, education, dress sense and organisational ability she knew she was quite good too. How on earth had Halima been able to make Bala fall in love with her? Would he have done so if she, Muni, had not insisted on their separation and subsequent divorce? He had been bitter about her decision at the time. She was quite certain that if she had not ended the marriage, he would not have fallen in love with Halima. Or would he? An idea came into her mind.

Heavens, no! She was not going to try and get him back so that they could remarry. She and Ladi loved each other and she would not really want to live with Bala again. Still, how comforting it would be to win him away from that girl and wipe that arrogant and self assured smile off her silly face. Muni would lead him on for a while and tell him it was all over. How deflated the great Bala would be!

Super! He would be too hurt to go crawling back to the girl who would be too proud to hang around or take him back after she had been dropped so unceremoniously in favour of an ex-wife. It did occur to her that he would have to get married someday, as she intended to herself, and she was not opposed to the idea, but her mind would be more at peace if he did not marry someone with whom he was very much in love. She did not want any woman to displace her children in their father's affection. Therefore, Halima posed a threat. You did not tell me that Muni is very beautiful, Halima told Bala that evening. Is she? Anyway, you never asked me.

I met her today and I was quite impressed by her personality. He did not make any comment. Won't you ask me where? You met her at her brother's when your Hausa class went there for coffee. Who told you? Your driver. Inuwa? Why did you ask him where we had been? I don't ask him such questions but I don't

stop him if he has anything to tell me. Hmm! I
didn't know I had spies all around me. Perhaps
he felt the incident was worth mentioning.
Katinka said that Muni is doing a marvelous job
at the Children's Home.

Is she? He sounded bored. Don't you
agree? That she's doing a wonderful job? Yes.
You sound uninterested. He brightened up.
Smart girl! How did you guess? I am
uninterested! I've not come here to discuss
Muni. I've missed you all day and after the
lovely supper you"ve just given me, I'm
waiting for something to digest it.

What?

Your kisses, darling, what else? he said as
his arms went around her. Some weeks later
Halima got a letter from the Children's Home
asking if she could please spare an hour three
times a week to give oral lessons in French to

some of the children who were being sponsored by a philanthropist on a four week holiday in Niamey in the neighbouring Republic of Niger. Her selfless services in the State, the letter went on, were widely acknowledged and appreciated and the management of the Home was certain that she would be willing to help these underprivileged children whose trip would be made much easier if they had a little foreknowledge of the language and culture of the country they were going to visit. The letter was signed by Muni Sumiyar.

Halimar loved children and would have been very glad to help out but she did not want anything that would bring her into contact with Bala's ex-wife. She no longer disliked her as she had done before meeting her, but she did not see what use an association with her could be. Go and help out, Halima, advised Rahila when she heard of the request. You know you'll never forgive yourself if you don't

Okay, but why did she choose me for the job? She must have something up her sleeve. She looked at me with concealed hate in her eyes when we met. Besides, there must be lots of people she could contact who would be glad to help. Her sister-in-law speaks French fluently.

Katinka might have other engagements or might not have a flair for teaching children. Anyway, it's a temporary thing, isn't it? Yes, just four weeks, according to the letter. Apart from the first day, when Muni introduced her to the children and the staff at the Home, they hardly saw each other, and on the last day she turned up to thank her and have one of the children present a gift to her. Halima had enjoyed giving lessons to the children, but she declined politely when Muni suggested that she helped out with English lessons. In another setup she would have obliged, but she knew she would not really be quite comfortable having such frequent contact with her. Bala, surprisingly, tried to urge her to accept and she found this funny since he had initially been against the idea of her going to help at the Home.

She could not help noticing too that the relationship between him and his ex-wife had become more cordial. His driver turned up at the Home on one errand or the other when Halima was there for lessons and he used to park at a place where she could not fail to notice him. Muni, who had obviously sent for him, made a show of getting in or out of the car, or of giving him elaborate last minute instructions. She made sure that her voice carried as far as Halima's classroom. The latter refrained from asking Bala what the game was. She knew how he hated her to be jealous of his association with other people. She was angry, however, when Muni's driver began to deliver notes for Bala at her place.

Don't worry, darling, he told her when she asked him what was going on. These notes are usually about things the girls want me to get for them. Here, read this. She read the note. What's so urgent about it that it cannot be sent to your house or your office? You speak to your daughters almost every day, couldn't they ask you themselves? And what's this "Bala darling stuff for? If you both desire to get together again for whatever purpose, you can do so with a lot more finesse. These days she seems bent on making me know that you were once married to her. Oh, come off it, Halima, he chided gently. Even when we are married Muni will still communicate with me. She's the mother of my children.

How she wished he had not said that bit. It

made her acutely jealous. She too would one day be the mother of his children. Had she been foolish in postponing their wedding? Should she really wait until the following year? What was she waiting for anyway? She could not say. It was as if she was waiting to fulfil something. An ambition? What ambition? At twenty five she ought to be more definite about what she wanted. She envied women like Muni and Rahila who seemed to be well sorted out. Perhaps she should go for further studies. Should she do a postgraduate course in Business Administration? By the end of the course she should be more purposeful about the future. Or should she get married and have claims on Bala? She was uneasy about his revival of interest in Muni. Did he still care for his ex-wife?

Muni invited us to her sister's wedding in Funtua. Here's the card, Bala told her one evening. Will you be going? she asked curiously.

Yes, of course. Saratu used to spend her holidays with Muni and me. She was like a younger sister to me. Cute girl with nice manners. You'll like her. I'm not attending the wedding, Bala. Why not? You're invited. Stop and think for a moment, darling. How would you expect me to feel in the midst of your ex-wife's relatives? Now that you're both on sweet terms, I can imagine how she'd carry on, dragging you all over the place, reintroducing you to forgotten in-laws and friends, reminding you of past incidents and occasions. In short, anything designed to make me feel like an outsider. I'm surprised that you are prepared to subject me to such an ordeal. Muni will do nothing of the sort. She's more friendly now because she's realised that you mean a lot to me. She's always telling me what a nice person you are.

I have my suspicions about her motives for that. Anyway, I don't have to be at this wedding. If it were one of your daughters getting married, I would attend of course, but.. I see your point even though I still think your fears are groundless. I'll be away for the weekend. All of it? The main ceremony is taking place on Saturday morning. Couldn't you drive back straight after it? Surely you're not going to stay behind for the merrymaking that follows? I thought Muni, I mean the girls, might need me around.

Whatever for? What important roles are they playing that necessitate your presence after the main ceremony?

Er, actually I thought they could spend some time with me in my family house so that they could see a bit of their grandparents and the rest of the family. Fair enough, she agreed, although she failed to see why his presence was needed for this. The girls were growing up and they visited their grandparents at least five times a year. However, not wanting the matter to develop into an argument, she dropped it altogether. She missed him badly that weekend and that got her thinking seriously about their relationship and the future. She admitted to herself for the first time that she had lost her individuality.

She spent all Saturday moping and thinking and by evening she had come to a conclusion about her social life. She was going to develop more outside interests and not rely on Bala to provide her with distractions. That way she would not be at a loose end whenever he was not around.

So, when Rahila invited her over for supper with Usman, her boyfriend of two years, she did not hesitate about going there alone as she would have done in the past. If Bala could accept an invitation from his ex-wife she saw no reason why she should refuse one from a lifelong friend. She dug out a favourite trouser suit, matching handbag and shoes and left the house in a light mood, determined to enjoy herself. At the door she stopped. To liven up her mood further, she would drive herself to Rahila"s. She enjoyed driving. The feel of the driving wheel and the uplift of her hair in the wind always gave her a happy feeling. The sports car would be ideal. She would have to tell the driver that his services were not needed for the evening.

As soon as she stepped outside the door, he materialised from the guard"s hut and hurried over to her. Good evening, madam. What car do I bring out?

The sports car, please. Here let me have

the key. It was Bala's decision that the driver kept the keys to the cars. He explained that it made the driver loyal when he realised how much trust was put in him. You can have the evening off. I'll drive myself. Oh no, please, madam, the man cried, aghast at the idea. I go lose my job if my master knows that you drive yourself. He don gif me firm instructions about dat.

Don't worry, he won't mind. I'll tell him about it. Let me have the keys. Sorry, madam, he said uncomfortably, I can't. Halima felt exasperated but knew that further argument with him was pointless. Why had Bala issued such an instruction when he knew how much she loved to drive? Perhaps it was to make sure the driver did not shirk his duties on the pretext that she wanted to drive herself. He was a kind but strict employer. Here I go again trying to excuse his action, she scolded herself. For all she knew it could be a ploy to ensure that the driver knew all her movements and could report back to him. No, no, he would not stoop so low. Not her noble Bala. Still the thought remained with her all the way to Rahila's. Rahila looked radiant in a low cut, full sleeved buba and a wrapper made from the latest white lace material.

She had on a matching set of a pearl necklace, earrings and bracelets and the tresses of her long, woven hair framed her face giving her a sexy look. Usman had discarded his usual uniform of khaki tunic and trousers in favour of a complete set of agbada in the same material as hers. He was of average height and stockily built and could have looked attractive if he had taken more notice of what he wore. Halima sometimes wondered what yardstick her friend used when choosing her boyfriends for no two were ever alike. From all indications her search for an ideal companion seemed to be over for she and Usman fitted like old gloves. Apart from being fond of each other they were also very good friends.

They both had a happy satisfied look about them as they welcomed her warmly to their house. She was fixed a drink and told that three other people would be joining them for dinner. From the lounge where they sat she could see the dining table laid prettily out with a new cloth, flowers and candles. There were flowers on the sideboard too. She was surprised. Normally, Rahila had no time for such decorations, not even when she entertained local celebrities, which was often. She preferred to pay more attention to the food and drinks, arguing that that was what most guests were likely to remember of the occasion. Something was definitely in the air, Halima decided. Her friend, who was looking softer and more subdued than usual, had been avoiding her gaze since she arrived and the garrulous Usman had suddenly become tongue tied. She glanced from one to the other.

All right you two, she said suddenly, the game's up. What have you been up to? Robbed a bank? Kidnapped a millionaire's child? Out with it, my dear. Mother's listening. Em, er, began Usman. Furtive glances were exchanged between him and Rahila. Come on, come on, coaxed Halima. Surely you can take an old friend like me into your confidence. I won't tell Interpol. What are you celebrating? It's a celebration, isn't it? Well, it is, admitted Rahila a bit uncomfortably and since your crystal ball has told you that much . . . Shall we tell her? she asked Usman. The announcement was to be the highlight of the evening.

Look, my precious two. I'll walk out right away if you don't tell me, Halima threatened and not all the gold or diamonds in the world would ever make me speak to you again. Okay, tell her Rahila.

We got married yesterday.

Why, this is great news!" cried Halima, jumping to her feet and rushing over to kiss first Rahila, then Usman, and Rahila again. „Who else have you invited for dinner?" she asked.

Usman's brother, Dauda, and his wife Becky. They asked if they could bring along a guest of theirs as they couldn't leave him behind all on his own. I've met him; a very boring and conceited man. What's his name, er, er, darling, what's the name of Dauda's guest? Paddy Bello. Yes, Paddy. He talks about nothing else but his conquests with women and his success as a Public Relations Consultant in Lagos. I'm surprised he was able to come down here for the weekend. Judging by the way he talks you"d think that all activities in Lagos would grind to a halt if he dared leave the place. I find him quite pleasant, said Usman. He's highly intelligent.

Darling, you like anyone who shares your political ideologies. Naturally, he laughed. Halima did not find Paddy boring and conceited. She liked his affable manners. He was short, a bit hefty with a rugged ugly face, but with his muscular, hairy chest, which he seemed to leave permanently exposed, his smart, blown out afro hair cut and his tasteful mode of dressing, there was a maleness about him which made him very attractive and interesting, particularly to the opposite sex. He was aware of this, and he treated every woman with respect, showering her with compliments and making her feel important and pretty.

As soon as he saw Halima that evening he pounced on her as if she had been invited purposely to form a twosome with him. She played along and they chatted like old friends. Later, a friend who had got wind of the wedding rang to invite all of them to a nightclub. Out of mischief, or perhaps to get even with her driver for refusing to give her the key to the car, she decided not to make use of his services for the journey. She did not want him tailing them either so she slipped through a side door and joined Rahila and Usman in their car a short distance down the road and they roared off, giggling like naughty school children.

She sighed contentedly as she sat in the tightly packed room and looked forward to an enjoyable evening. It was lovely to be one of the crowds instead of sitting at a high table making polite conversations with some dull dignitaries, as was usually the case when she and Bala went out. They never went to nightclubs or swinging parties. Well, she was not crazy about these either, and she rather enjoyed the special attention they got wherever they went as guests but life did seem a bit monotonous sometimes.

She felt young and happy as she danced with Paddy, wriggling and jumping to disco music. Nearby, Rahila and Usman were neatly merged together, hardly moving, oblivious of the beat of the music, or of anything else for that matter. People relaxed in their chairs and watched as the dancers waltzed gracefully and expertly. When the music stopped there was a prolonged ovation. The band struck up a tango and the dancers continued. Shall we join them? Paddy asked Halima as they watched.

Sorry, she replied. I don't understand these steps. It was a lie as she was itching to join in the dancing as the band played a popular tango number, but she could not bring herself to do it with a stranger and in a nightclub. She thought wistfully of Bala and what he might be doing at that moment.

Muni went to bed that Saturday night after a very hectic day feeling exhausted and extremely unhappy. She had been the chief organiser for the wedding reception and the various parties which had followed. Everything had gone successfully, and a good time had been had by all except herself. Her personal plans, carefully nursed over several weeks, had failed to bring about the anticipated results.

The first and most painful blow had been the refusal of Moukta, her fiancé, to stay on after the wedding ceremony which had taken place in the morning. He had marched off at the head of the busload of friends he had brought along, saying he had too much pride to hang around and watch her make an ass of herself over her ex-husband. He had accused her of thoughtlessly involving Bala in all the major activities while he, who was supposed to be the important man in her life, had been left to assume the role of an onlooker. He had been highly embarrassed to notice his fiancée confer with her ex-husband over every detail.

She had been full of remorse and had offered heartfelt apologies, but the damage had been done. She could not ask Bala to stop carrying out the duties he had been assigned. Moukta had left to entertain his friends in Zaria since they had dropped everything else to spend the weekend with him.

Muni had arranged things the way she did to spite Halima — who did not turn up. This had been her second blow. She had wanted to show her how much hold she still had over Bala and make her aware that any wife or children he acquired would always take second place to their daughters in his affection. She was convinced that if Halima saw how involved he was with members of her family the point would be rammed home firmly. She had not thought of what effect her plan would have on Moukta and his reaction had shocked her. She became irritated each time Bala came near her and by evening they were hardly on speaking terms as he too had become cross and moody.

Bala had been surprised when Muni had told him how involved he was going to be in the wedding celebrations. He had thought of showing up with Halima at the reception to give the newlyweds a present and from there going to enjoy a quiet weekend in Katsina. Instead the role of master of ceremony and principal coordinator had been thrust upon him by Muni. Well, he had done his bit and he hoped he had done it well. He decided to give the night party a miss so that he could drive straight back to Kaduna and give Halima a pleasant surprise.

He was surprised when he arrived at

Halima's place and was told by her housekeeper that she was out. Out at a half past one in the morning? Where? With whom? He looked in the garage and noticed the absence of the sports car. He knew how much she loved to drive it. Had she gone out alone? He beckoned to the night guard who hurried over to explain that she had left with the driver. He went indoors to wait. By two o'clock all his nerves were on edge. He went to the study and tried to meditate. It was useless, he could concentrate on nothing. He began to pace the room. Where was Halima? She could not be at her parents" or at Rahila's at that time of the morning. Had there been a crisis? There could not have been as the housekeeper had told him that she had left the house looking quite cheerful. And if there had been an accident, the household would have been informed. He did not want to raise an alarm by ringing round at that hour to find out where she was. Already, there was panic in the eyes of her small staff who had huddled together in a comer talking in dejectedly low tones, refusing to go to bed without knowing what had happened to their mistress.

As the night wore on he became annoyed by their whisperings and he firmly sent them off to bed. Some minutes later he heard the car in the driveway. He hurried to the door and yanked it open. On seeing Bala, Halima was so overcome with sheer delight that she threw elegance aside, dashed out of the car, ran up the steps and threw herself into his outstretched arms. The night guard and the driver exchanged grins as the couple clung together and Bala had to walk backwards into the house. She was bursting with love and pride that he had driven down that night to be with her.

Seeing the immense joy and affection in her eyes, a great tenderness swept through him, overcoming all the wild suspicions and jealousy that had sprouted inside him. Well, almost. That whiff of a male aftershave that clung to her cheek? Where was it from? A man? It had to be, after all she had just explained to him that she. had been at an impromptu outing to celebrate Rahila and Usman"s wedding plans. Curse them! Why had they thrown the damned thing when he was not around to accompany his girl? Who were the others at the gathering? He was too proud to ask Halima and she was too happy to indulge in such irrelevant details.

Actually the evening had become boring towards the end and Paddy's adoring glances and witty remarks had ceased to interest her. She dozed in her chair and was relieved when someone noticed and suggested they left. The sports car was parked neatly in front of the nightclub and, as soon as she came out, her driver, who had been hovering at the entrance, sprang forward to lead her to it. Her companions, slightly drunk and in high spirits applauded such efficiency and dedication to duty with a loud laugh. They congratulated th6 driver on his marvelous detective job. Halima joined in the fun while inwardly wondering how the man knew that she had left Rahila"s and how he had been able to trace them. However, she asked no questions as they drove home and the incident soon slipped from her mind.

Chapter 3

As soon as he had handed Halima out of the car Inuwa got back in and drove off the way he had come. She was mildly surprised that he had not parked the car and gone to his rooms in the domestic quarters as he normally did at the end of the day. Could he be making off with the car? She laughed at such a ridiculous thought; the man had been working for Bala for more than eight years and was very trustworthy. He must have been asked to report back at Bala"s. What for, at that time of night? Well, she was far too happy that evening to allow such thoughts to bother her.

It had been her twenty sixth birthday and it had been celebrated in a unique way. Bala had given her a fantastic but rather unusual birthday party at the best hotel in town. About sixty friends and acquaintances were to be lavishly entertained until dawn or whenever they chose to leave. Special trays, mugs and handkerchiefs to commemorate the occasion were to be distributed. The party had been unusual because she and Bala had stayed for just one hour receiving the guests and then he had calmly announced that he and the celebrant were going to spend the evening on their own somewhere else. He wished everyone an enjoyable evening and they left. To say that Halima was surprised was an understatement. She had been absolutely thrown. She had looked forward to a pleasant evening after a day which had passed delightfully, and he had given no inkling at all about what he had in mind.

He had taken that day off work so that they could spend it together at his place. That had been odd too as they virtually lived in her house which was cosier and more intimate. They had spent the day simply and alone; he had given the domestic staff the day off.

They swam, played tennis, cards, records and Halima made lunch. They laughed and hugged, feeling very close. She enjoyed the way he followed her about the house, touching and kissing her unexpectedly. I've not bought any presents for you, precious, he told her afterwards as they sat in the garden. I decided not to. Oh, the party you're throwing for me is enough, darling, she told him happily. You've bought me so many things that I can't think of anything else you could possibly give me. I do have a present for you. She looked at him, puzzled. I thought you said The present I am giving you for your twenty sixth birthday, Halima, cannot be bought. It is my heart.

You've always had my love and now you'll have it for life, no matter what happens between us. He leaned back in his chair, eyes half closed, fingertips together as if in meditation. When he opened his eyes she could see a hint of sadness in them. She felt afraid and apprehensive. What was the matter? Was he going to die? Sometimes he was unfathomable. Soon, the moment passed. He smiled, sprang up from his chair and pulled her to her feet. Come on, let's go and get ready for the party. Race you to the house. Fine, she laughed as they set off.

It had taken her months of intensive search in the shops to come up with the dress and accessories she had on that night, and the look of admiration in Bala's eyes told her that the trouble had been worthwhile.

It was a long, clinging, sea green silk dress which accentuated her figure. The diamond studs in her ears, her luxuriant shoulder length jet black hair, light makeup, silver handbag and stiletto heeled silver shoes made an enchanting overall picture. My love, Bala said tenderly as they were about to leave. You look exquisite and I must record this image. He got out his camera and for the next twenty minutes was busy clicking away. When they left the birthday party he pulled her into his arms as the driver drove slowly through the almost deserted streets. She sighed and nestled contentedly against him. Where are we heading for? she asked in a whisper. Home and to bed, he whispered back. Where else? I couldn't bear sharing you all evening with that crowd back there.

She felt happy but there was a small nagging regret at the back of her mind that she had been deprived of her role as the star of the evening. All that dressing up somehow now seemed a waste of time and effort. This was forgotten later in his place as they made love passionately. If this is how life with Bala is going to be, she told herself on the way back to her house, then being married to him will be one long honeymoon. She fingered the envelope he had handed over to her while she was leaving and wondered what was inside.

A cheque? Love poems? Well, she'd soon know she told herself as she skipped lightly up the steps leading to the house. She fell in love with the whole world as she bent to sniff the fragrance of the "queen of the night", a flower that was in a pot on her verandah. She was surprised that her housekeeper, who usually waited up for her, had not opened the door.

She rang the bell, feeling slightly neglected. No one came to the door. She rang again and kept her finger on the bell. The sound vibrated throughout the house. She looked at her wristwatch — a quarter to one. Perhaps the woman had fallen asleep. No, she was too assiduous about her job to do that. Instead she would keep eating kola nuts to stimulate her and keep her awake. Could she have been taken ill and gone into a coma? Halima became panicky. For all she knew there was a corpse in there. The house seemed uncannily silent. She beckoned to the guard. As he drew nearer she noticed that it was not the regular one she had had since she moved into the house. She was astounded. Who are you? she asked him in Hausa.

Night guard, madam, he said nervously. Where's the usual one? she asked, trying to control the fear in her. I don't know, madam.

Who employed you?

Mister Sumiyar.

I see. It's all right then.

Bala had probably forgotten to tell her of

the change. Please go around to the domestic quarters and call somebody. I think my housekeeper has fallen asleep inside the house. There was no need to alarm the man yet. The door could be broken down if she could not get in through the back door. There's no one there, madam, said the man, not moving.

What do you mean there's no one? They've all moved out. I saw some of them leaving with their belongings this evening as I came on duty. They said the master told them to go. Go? Was the man drunk? Come with me. They went to the back of the building. She did not need to knock on any of the doors to know that the place was deserted. The absence of pots, pans and chairs on the verandah told the whole story. She felt as if she was in a dream. She shook her head. There must be an explanation. She would have to get into the house somehow and telephone Bala. She remembered that she had a key to a side door that she always carried in her purse. She prayed fervently that it was still there, and that the door was not barricaded from the inside. It was not and she got in, locking it carefully behind her and using the bolts. The guard turned away relieved and went back to his hut near the gate.

She switched on the lights and almost fainted at what she saw — or rather at what she did not see. The house had been completely stripped bare except for the curtains. Everything, right down to the floor mat in the kitchen had disappeared. She gathered up her dress and ran from room to room flinging doors open. It was the same story, everywhere was bare. She rubbed her eyes and laughed hysterically. There must be an explanation. Perhaps he had moved her to a larger place and it was meant to be a birthday surprise. That was it! He had always complained that the house was too small.

She ran to the phone and dialled Bala's number. A smile played on her lips as she pictured her domestic staff waiting eagerly for her in the new house. She could not get through. She called several times before it dawned on her that the phone was dead. She was puzzled. It had been working that morning. Had the P&T done their stuff again? She had no outstanding bills.

She thought hard. But would Bala really play such a joke on her? Leaving her stranded like that without a car and a driver to take her back to his house, or somewhere else? And at that time of the night? It was then she remembered the letter in her handbag. She got it out and began to read. She read it through once without registering anything. When she read it the second time, she went cold at the contents. Really shivering cold.

The letter read,

My precious Halima,

This is the end of our relationship. You have brought it about. Five and a half months ago, when I went to attend Saratu's wedding in Funtua, you went out to celebrate Rahila and Usman's wedding plans with some friends of theirs. That was perfectly in order and I did not mind too much that I was not around to accompany you. What I do mind was the fact that you purposely deceived your driver as to your whereabouts by sneaking through Rahila's back door to join the others in their car which they had parked around the comer, to go to a nightclub.

This was a most disappointing and undignified action from a lady I love more than life itself. By it you have lowered the esteem your driver had for both of us as he must have concluded that you had gone off to meet another man. Now, that's not my thought for I know how genuine and stable your love for me is. But I simply cannot forgive or forget this deception. It shows there's no future for us as husband and wife and I cannot have our relationship any other way. Why couldn't you let the driver know where you were off to? Try as I may not to show it, I will always doubt your words and actions and that's not good for any marriage. So, darling, we must part. It has taken me five months since I heard of the incident, and made my own investigations, to arrive at this decision.

As I said this afternoon I have given you my heart (which is now broken forever) and I can never love nor marry another woman. I have not turned you out of your house and disbanded your domestic staff out of cruelty. I simply cannot bear to see and touch the things we had shared so intimately together. I have burnt some property and sent others to charity bodies. Your boxes of clothes I have sent to your parents. Goodbye my only love.

Your Bala.

She read the letter again. His decision did not make any sense to her. Why could he not have discussed the matter with her? He agreed that he did not think that she had been unfaithful to him, yet he wanted to make her feel as if she had committed a grievous crime. Had he gone mad? She felt as if she too was going mad. Her harmless little prank had turned out to be quite expensive. Her mind went numb. She refused to think. She would become insane if she did.

She got up from the floor and yanked off some curtains to use as bedding. She put off the lights and lay down, willing death to come. It was the only logical answer to her problem and God would surely not refuse to grant her her wish. She was not going to take her own life. That was a sin, and a crime if she failed, but how could she possibly live without Bala?

Halima fell into a deep sleep and woke up

after midday. At first she was baffled by the unaccustomed hard bed, then she saw the letter and everything came rushing back. She was surprised that she was still alive. She read the letter again, but this time dispassionately. She got up, stretched, and went to the window. There was no doubt her heart was broken and she felt somehow used, but she was young and resilient enough to take the cruel knocks that life handed out periodically.

She loved Bala very much but, if she lived to be a thousand, she would never comprehend why he had had to break off their relationship in such a sadistic and spectacular way. How more cruel can a human being be? An outright quarrel and a final parting would have been a lot kinder and more humane. That side to his character was what shocked her more than the loss of her property. That had been her fault. If she had listened to Rahila and not allowed herself to be 'kept' by Bala, she would have her own flat and property and would have had only the problem of nursing a broken heart. The situation would not now be so humiliating. She had learnt her lesson. But at what a cost.

The sound of passing cars and the noise of children playing next door filled the afternoon air and she felt very much alive. She went to the bathroom to wash her face, giving silent thanks that Bala had not removed the taps or stopped the water supply. Suddenly she saw a lighter side to the situation and gave a short laugh. She let herself out of the house, locked the side door and threw the key into the shrubs. A part of her had died that moment and she knew it. Her heart ached but she was ready to take her life into her own hands and face the future. Ignoring the guard at the gate and the curious stares of the neighbours, who must all be aware of her plight, she hailed a taxi for her parents.

By the time she got there her iron resolve had melted and her spirits had sunk again. Her body ached from the night she had spent on the floor. She was tired and there was this great emptiness in her heart. The tears would not even come. They came cascading down however when she stepped out of the taxi and her mother rushed forward to fold her in her arms, her face suffused with worry and anxiety. She rocked her in her arms and led her into the house while her father came out to settle the fare.

I had your room cleaned out and made ready, her mother told her as they entered the room Halima had not used for the past four years. Everything was as she had left it. She noticed her five suitcases neatly arranged in a comer. When did these arrive? she asked. Yesterday afternoon. Your driver said Bala told him to bring them here. It was odd, because you had not said anything about it when you rang in the morning to thank us for your birthday present. I knew nothing about it until I got back from Bala's at midnight, she said brokenly. She had stopped sobbing now and seemed drained of all emotions. Her hunger pangs had disappeared. Her father came into the room and sat by his wife on the sofa. Halima sat on the chair by her bed fiddling with the bedspread. We tried to reach you by phone but couldn't, her mother said. He had had the telephone disconnected. And when your father went round to your place he was told that you had left for Bala's in the morning and were going to be away all day. There was silence. Do you want to talk about it?

She nodded and in a quiet voice narrated the events of the previous day and handed over Bala's letter. They read it.

Go on, Mum, say it, Halima said wearily.

Say, "I told you so". No, my daughter, I will not. We all make mistakes. You've suffered enough. I can imagine what you've been through, she added gently. Your love, faith and pride have all taken a beating. As a woman, I understand. She went and put her arms around her daughter. Mr Kadizu left them together. Haliru took the first available plane down from Jos two days later. He had been furious when his father had told him over the telephone of Halima's ordeal and he was boiling with rage now at the family meeting they were holding on the issue. Halima sat quietly listening to their views and trying to sort out her feelings. She had had time for a little self appraisal and had had to admit that she Had been the world's most stupid female. She deserved a medal for foolishness and lack of foresight. She had given up almost everything she had for Bala"s love and in return he had kicked dust in her face, making her the laughing stock of the town. She was going to steer her own course in future, as she had always intended to before she fell in love. So, when she was asked her plans, she did not hesitate.

I'm going into politics, she announced to her astonished family. Politics! they exclaimed in unison, thinking they had not heard right. Think carefully, Halima, advised her father. You've had a rough deal from a man you loved and trusted and if I may hazard a guess you probably want to go into politics to champion the cause of women in one way or the other.

You're right, Dad, she agreed quietly. In this country women are downtrodden and taken for granted, and they calmly accept their lot, attributing it to the dictates of nature. They hardly have any rights. I agree, but go carefully. I can see your mind's made up and knowing how strong willed you are, you're not likely to change it. I won't. Women are hardly represented at federal or state level and as such no one thinks of doing anything to improve their status. The few female legislators there have their views snuffed out of them before they have an opportunity to air them. That's true, agreed her mother. The Press does not help either. They would rather focus their attention on what the female legislators wore to the House of Assembly than on what contributions they made to the debates. The men in the room maintained a diplomatic silence.

And when they condescend to do this, said Halima, they report in such a way as to make the female member's contributions seem childish and ineffective, thereby making the masses come to the conclusion that electing women into the House of Assembly or the Senate was a waste of votes. Men in this country are out to suppress the women in every way they can. Here she was thinking of Bala and Malam Sani.

I would say men all over the world are trying to do that, said Mrs Kadizu. It's just that in some countries, the women are not taking it lying down. They are doing something. Would you want to contest the next general elections?

Why not? They come up in two years time and by then I ought to have consolidated my position within a Party. Luckily I'm in a state capital and, as I intend to start at state level, it should be easy to get recognised and appreciated if I work hard. What about money? I'll pick up a job, she said with a bitter smile. My glorious days as a "kept" lady are over. There was silence and then they each got up to kiss her and wish her luck. There was some apprehension in their minds however as to whether she had made the right decision and if she was resilient enough to survive in the world of politics.

And now, announced Haliru quietly as he brought a knife from the folds of his garment, drew it out of its sheath and felt the sharp edge, I'll go and kill Bala.

There was a startled silence. His father was the first to recover. Haliru, what's the meaning of this? Did we bring you up to become a murderer? His mother and sister began to sob. He ignored them, replaced the knife in its sheath and put it back in his pocket. He picked up the keys to the family car and strode towards the front door. His father barred his way. Haliru, do you want to send your mother and me to our graves? Bala deserves to die, said Haliru with a mad gleam in his eyes. He's disgraced my family and the only honourable thing for me to do is to kill him, for I'll never be able to live down the way he's treated my sister. You're in the twentieth century you know, said his father. It's a sin and a crime to kill.

I don't care. Haliru tried to force his way past his father, who quickly realised that his approach was wrong and wheedling would be more effective. Listen, my son, he said, placing a hand on Haliru's shoulder. There's no doubt that Bala deserves whatever treatment you have in mind for him, but let us ponder a bit. Will killing him rectify the harm that has already been done? Will it not bring further dishonour to this family to have one of its members branded a killer? There's a death sentence or life imprisonment too. Think of your wife Laraba and your young son — and of course your parents and your sister.

I've thought carefully about all that and I've made a will. No one will suffer financially if I'm condemned to death, he told them. I cannot allow Bala to go scot free. He has the right to end his relationship with Halima, but not the way he did it; exposing my family to ridicule; asserting that because he's wealthy he can behave anyhow and get away with it. I must kill him. He tried to get past his father. His mother stepped forward and flung herself at him. You'll have to kill me first then, Haliru, because I cannot bear to lose my son in such a foolish manner. I love you too much to want to continue living if you're hanged or sentenced to life imprisonment. Bala would be laughing in his grave because of the trouble and humiliation we would be subjected to by your killing him. And, in the long run, he'd be the victor. Now, Haliru, I ask you, why concede further victory to a man who has behaved so abominably?

Haliru said nothing as he tried to disengage himself from her, but she held him more tightly and asked him for the knife. Halima was sitting staring in front of her as if in a trance. She looked so dejected and unhappy that Haliru's fury melted, giving way to pity for her. He had been mainly concerned about the family''s honour and had not given any thought to what she must have gone through and would still have to go through. In short he''d been most selfish.

He hugged his mother, handed over the knife and went to sit by his sister who began to weep silently, agony racking her body. He put his arms round her and tried to soothe her as she apologised for the trouble she had brought to the family.

What's the matter, Halima? Rahila asked one evening when the former walked into the room where she was running up a dress for one of her children. You look dreadful. Tiredness I can understand and attribute to the hard work at the factory, but the sadness which has been absent from your eyes for the past three weeks is back. Rahila was very observant when she was fond of someone.

Halima had been working for her as Production/Marketing Manager at the garment factory for about six weeks. It was grueling work. For some unknown reason Halima had always had the impression that Rahila led a cushioned life running between the factory and the hotel merely supervising the workers. Now, she could not imagine how she had managed singlehandedly before Usman joined her. Halima found the job so demanding and was kept so busy that, at the end of each day, all she could manage during the first two weeks were a bath, a meal and then it was blissful sleep. There was no time for anything else but to look forward to another action packed day. The routine suited her and in a way she was happy. She deliberately blocked out any thoughts of Bala.

She lived in a tiny chalet in the grounds of

Rahila's hotel. She had insisted on independence as soon as she got her job, refusing to live either with her parents or with Usman and Rahila in their flat in the main building of the hotel. Actually, she would have preferred living elsewhere but Rahila had insisted that accommodation went with the job, and that if she rejected it, the offer of appointment would be withdrawn.

She had been a bit angry at the time that her close friend was being so businesslike about the job. She had not been pleased either about the way Rahila had shown indifference about her broken romance, not wanting to discuss it, pretending not to notice that she was pining away for Bala's love.

So far, everyone had been concerned about her finding her feet, settling down to a job or a career. No word of sympathy about her ruined relationship had been forthcoming. Or did they think she had stopped loving him because of what had taken place? There was no question of ever going back to him, and she would marry someone else and raise a family so as to conform to society rules, but she knew that no man would ever replace him in her heart.

As she looked at Rahila now she was envious. The lady looked so fulfilled. She was well off, had a loving husband, smashing kids and glowed with good health in this new pregnancy. But she had earned it all and deserves this happiness, Halima conceded. She lived on the breadline for a while, but struggled and worked hard to survive. More importantly, she has got over all the traumas her second marriage brought her and has come out tops. Will I survive my heartache? I'll just have to.

What sort of day did you have? asked Rahila, seeing that her first question had gone unanswered. Busy but interesting as usual. I made some lovely kuka soup this afternoon and my nanny is making some tuwo. Have supper with us.

No, thanks, Rahila. Halima forced herself to smile. If her friend had her way she would feed her nonstop. She and Usman kept complaining that she was too thin. She usually had a good appetite but recently she had begun to feel queasy in the stomach and the smell of food made it worse. I know precisely what I'll have for supper tonight and that does not include any mouth watering kuka soup and tuwo, she said humorously, trying to stifle the envy she had felt earlier on. What are you going to have?

Nothing. I'll have a leisurely bath, read a bit and sleep. I'm not hungry tonight. Rahila was mildly surprised and a tiny bit worried. Halima usually skipped lunch during the week so she could indulge in huge, delicious suppers.

Halima, Rahila asked quietly, tell me what's wrong. Nothing. I'm expecting a baby, Halima said in a whisper.

Rahila, who was never one to control her emotions, was thrown into confusion. She flung down the garment she was hemming and turned round to stare at her friend wide eyed. Are you sure? When did this happen? Who's responsible? How old is it? Halima spoke quietly. Bala and I ... Well, we were going to get married later this year ... I hadn't noticed that I had missed ... I suppose because of my state of mind at the time. So, it must be just over two months old. I see. Does Bala know?

No, I don't intend to tell him, and I forbid anyone to do so. Yes, yes, of course. What are you going to do? It's obvious, isn't it? It'll have to come off. Oh, Halima, how can you? cried the other aghast. You can't possibly want to.

Abortion! That's murder! My goodness! It's not a question of what I want, it is a question of what I have to do. Why should I bring a child into the world when the father has rejected me and thrown me out on the flimsy excuse that I did not allow my driver to take me to my destination? How would he react to news of my pregnancy? Do you want me involved in a paternity suit? Bala wouldn't disown the pregnancy. He'd be thrilled at the news. He loves you so much. I have my reservations about that. However, abortion is the only solution. I've discussed the matter with my mother and, like you, she's against my decision, but it's my life, you know. I'm the central figure in this drama.

Rahila did not agree, and, long after her friend had left, she abandoned her work and was plunged into her thoughts. How she wished Halima had not confided in her. Ignorance was such a blissful state in such a situation. Now, she would have to try to live with her conscience as an associate murderer. Oh dear Allah! Halima might lose her life through the abortion even though she had said Haliru had recommended a good doctor in Jos. Did Haliru support the termination of the pregnancy? Perhaps like her, he had no choice but to accept it. What could she do? She could not share her full anxiety with her husband who had already told her that for Halima to fully recover from her sad experience, she should be allowed to steer her own life.

That weekend Halima had made up her mind about which Party to join — the Social Reformer's Party. Its major objectives were: equal opportunity for everyone, particularly women; shortening the wide gap between the rich and the poor, thereby giving every citizen the right to a good useful life; putting the nation first; free education and health services and cheap housing schemes for the lower and middle income cadre. These fell in line with what she had in mind. She thought it was smart of the Party to place emphasis on the rights of women who were the majority in the country. If the majority of the women could be reached and their votes secured, then the Party would have one or two states to govern after the next elections. It had none at the moment.

Halima resolved to work hard when she joined so she could rise to a prominent position from which she could realise some of the reforms she had in mind. There was no notable female leader yet at state or national level and she hoped to fill that void.

Come and keep me company this afternoon, Halima darling, Rahila asked her one Saturday morning when she called on her way to the shops. I shall be all alone. Usman's away on one of his tiresome political campaigns. The children are going to a birthday party. Shall we say five o'clock? Okay, fine. I will be through with my chores by then, agreed Halima, although she did wonder why a particular time had to be fixed for the visit.

It was with a light heart that she walked into Rahila's sitting room at a few minutes past five. Her friend was nowhere to be seen but Bala was there resplendent in immaculate white robes. He got up when she came in and walked hesitant towards her when she stopped dead on seeing him.

Her heart did cartwheels but outwardly she was very calm and cool, even haughty as she regarded him, as if looking at a stranger. She looked quizzically at him. His arms dropped to his sides.

Halima darling, he said, but this time he

stayed where he was, discouraged by her coldness. Come to me, my love. Bala, what do you want? She had decided not to walk out of the room. That would be rude and childish even though it was difficult to look at him and not rush into his arms, but she would do it. It would be a good way of finding out if she could face life without his love. She was not intending to hide away or spend the rest of her life dreading meeting him. There was no doubt that Rahila had arranged this meeting as a sort of therapy. Her heart warmed to her friend.

What do I want, my darling? he asked in a voice that would melt iron in the Arctic Circle. You, of course. I've come for you. The conceited chauvinist pig! He had thrown her out when he wanted to and now he had the effrontery to say that he had come for her, and it was when he wanted that, too.

Several retorts sprang to her mind but she

killed them, determined to be cold and distant so she could win the battle. What do you want, Bala? she asked as if she had not heard him. He was a bit put out by her coldness, but went bravely on. Come back to me, Halima. I can't live without you. I've tried to, but it gets harder each day. I love you so much. Dare I ask for forgiveness?

Halima refused to be drawn into an argument. As far as she was concerned Bala did not come into her programme at all, despite the yearning in her heart. She was going to be strong and survive without him. What do you want, Bala? she asked again, her voice rising this time. He was disappointed. He had not actually expected her to rush into his arms but he had not anticipated such an icy reception. Er, shall we sit down? I won't, but you can if you like. It"s not my house and I have not invited you here. In fact, I"m visiting myself. Standing made conversation difficult, but he could not sit down while she remained standing. Er, Rahila asked me to come.

I see. She accompanied this with a shrug of the shoulders to indicate that it was none of her business who Rahila invited to her house.

Er . . . er ... she told me about the baby. What baby? she asked lightly, her calm exterior cloaking the tumult inside her. Rahila! Oh, treacherous Rahila! How could you?! Our baby, precious! His eyes were glowing with pride and excitement.

Our baby she asked in an indifferent tone.

The one you're expecting. Rahila was kind enough to tell me about it. I shall go and see your parents when I leave here, and tomorrow I shall fly to see Haliru in Vom. I shall ask for his forgiveness too and we shall get married. Oh, my darling, this is marvellous news. She said nothing, looking at him as if waiting for him to go on. Bala became uncertain. Halima, please say something. I'm sorry, Bala, I don't know what you're talking about. Do you deny you're expecting our baby? Of course she could not. I was, she announced in a freezing tone, but I got rid of it some days ago. I had an abortion.

She had not and was still pregnant, but she knew it was better to tell him she had had the pregnancy terminated than that she was going to, and thereby avoid an argument on the subject Now it was a closed issue. Just like their relationship. She was totally unprepared for his explosive reaction.

You did what? he shouted, looking wildly around as if for a stick with which to beat her. He advanced threateningly on her. She backed away towards the door and fled from the room. You murderer, murderer, he hurled after her. I'll sue you in court for this. You"ll hang for killing my child.

Rahila rushed in through the other door, alarmed. His voice could be heard all over the flat. What's the matter? Where's Halima? She's killed our baby, he muttered softly as if speaking to himself. Our flesh and blood, our very first child, the fruit of our wonderful love. How could she? How could she have an abortion? How heartless and cruel! He subsided into a chair, his thoughts faraway. Rahila sat in another chair, not knowing what to do or say.

She felt sorry for the man. There was nothing else she could do. She had done the best she could in the circumstances. After a while he pulled himself together enough to thank her for her kind gesture, and he left, the figure of a broken man.

Despite the couple of sleeping tablets he

had taken, sleep eluded him that night. He tossed and turned, aching in mind and body. His anger and feeling of frustration at what Halima had done subsided enough and gave way to deep unhappiness. He ho longer blamed her for the step she had taken. After the cruel and disgraceful manner in which he had broken up their relationship he could hardly expect her to keep the pregnancy and thus maintain links with him. His offer of marriage in the circumstances had been ridiculous too. How could she ever consider such a proposal? It was an insult and he was surprised that she had not given him a slap for it. He had regretted breaking up with her the morning after it had happened.

He would have done anything to withdraw his letter, and had stayed by the telephone during the next three days in the hope that she would contact him and he could go rushing to her side. He had not dared to contact her. How could one explain that it was an insane jealousy that had nurtured such monstrous behaviour? She had not contacted him and depression had set in. The phone call from Rahila had been a lifesaving line and news of the pregnancy had sent him into unbelievable raptures. His dreams had now been dashed and, he vowed, he was through with love and marriage.

He thought of the first time they had made love, months after they had met. The joy and the wonder that he had been her very first lover had been overwhelming. It had made him more deeply in love with her, even though it would not have mattered if she had had other lovers before him. She had explained her virginity away simply, saying that she had always wanted that first experience to be with someone she cared deeply for. He had been flattered that she had chosen him to be that someone.

Well, all he looked forward to now was

work, work, work, to mask this great pain in his heart. When she got to her chalet that evening Halima collapsed into a chair, her feelings all mixed up. She was not angry, or sad. It had been wonderful seeing Bala again, and if he had walked in at that moment, abuses and all, she would have flung herself into his arms and told him that all was well and they could go ahead and get married. Yes, she would have swallowed her pride just to be with him again.

Later, she was glad he had not come after her. She despised herself for her weak and compromising thoughts. Where was this iron resolve of hers? It was there all right. She would have to exercise it. In a way, she had, hadn't she? After all, she had not gone running back to him. So, she was strong.

As the days went by, recalling the agony on his face at the news of the abortion acted as a balm on her bruised heart. The punishment was small in comparison with the hurt he had caused her, but it was something. She knew he would grieve about the loss of that pregnancy all the days of his life.

Chapter 4

After her encounter with Bala, Halima decided not to settle in Kaduna and run the risk of another one. It would disturb her peace of mind and she really did want to concentrate on politics. So she left for Jos and moved into a two bedroom flat Haliru had got for her. It was sparsely furnished from the little money she had, but for the first time in her life she felt delightfully free and independent. Every little item she bought gave her pleasure and a sense of achievement.

To have more time for her political activities, she opted for a part time job as an executive secretary with a French mining company. Her job mainly involved translation of documents so she brought work home with her and could work at her own pace. To make things easier she learnt to type and bought a typewriter. Most afternoons and evenings she spent at the state headquarters of the Social Reformers Party. Usman had given her good recommendations and she had been welcomed warmly into the fold. Actually he had cheated a bit saying that she had been a very good friend to the Party for some years but had only recently become a member because she had been away studying.

The first six months were a whirlwind of activities as she attended meetings, political rallies and campaigns. Whatever she had imagined the life of a politician to be, it certainly was not this rigorous one that consumed so much time and energy. How did the politicians ever find time for their own business? Due to her keen interest she was made a member of the action committee which was made up of fiercely dedicated young men and women. They met every week to discuss and weigh the merits and demerits of the states controlled by the other two political parties. At first she humorously referred to the meetings as gossipy since they sometimes discussed the latest scandals involving top government and company functionaries.

Later she discovered that it was a serious affair because these pieces of information were carefully sifted, analysed and investigated by an inner group and filed away to be used at press conferences and at political rallies. It made her feel like a member of the secret police. She was impressed by the amount of close monitoring that went on in each state and the correlation between the states and the Party's national headquarters in Lagos. She was surprised that a Party that was run on a shoestring budget should be so efficiently organised. This convinced her that there were still some Nigerians to whom money was not everything.

There was a monthly bulletin which reported faithfully all the Party's activities in each state. So you could walk into any secretariat and acquaint yourself with what was going on in other branches. The annual convention of the Party took place that year in Jos and Halima was very involved in the hectic preparations for it. Since she seemed to have more free time than many of the other members, most of the arrangements for transport, accommodation and entertainment were shoved on to her. She had not minded it because it gave her the opportunity to get acquainted with members from the other states and get more recognition at a higher level. She worked so hard that she collapsed on the second day of the weeklong convention. She was rushed to the hospital and Haliru was sent for. He was furious with her for not heeding his earlier advice of taking things easy.

When she felt better, he took her home to Danso where his wife Laraba could look after her. Halima, he told her one evening, the doctor has ordered a complete rest of at least six months for you. No work, no political activities.

Six months! she exclaimed feebly. That's too much. I don't need more than three months, really. I should be fit and strong by then if all goes well and I''ll resume my activities. You're doing nothing of the kind, and please none of your stubbornness. You'll stay here quietly for the next six months and, when you're pronounced fit by the doctor, you'll go back to Jos. Not a moment before. You've become a workaholic and are driving yourself into the grave, as if on purpose. Please, if you're contemplating suicide through unreasonably hard work, kindly go and do it on another planet where I won't know about it. Halima laughed and tried feebly to stand and give a salute. Yes, sir, she said, collapsing into her chair again. Ah right bro, your point is noted. And taken? he asked sternly.

Yes, and taken. She really felt drained. The doctor had told her that she had been lucky. Her condition on admission had been critical. She would have to be sensible and careful about things henceforth. Still, to her, six months was a long time. She would be forgotten by her employers and the members of the SRP, and would have to start all over again. Haliru, won't I be a burden to you and Laraba? You have your jobs and child and soon there'll be another. Can't I spend part of the six months in Jos where I have a good housekeeper?"

So you could throw yourself right back into the hub of things? No, you'll stay here. Do me a favour, will you? What's it? Stop whining about being a burden to Laraba and me.

Hear, hear, concurred Laraba, coming in from the kitchen with the baby strapped on to her back. They were followed by the maid carrying a steaming bowl of rice tuwo. Saliu, a cousin of Laraba's, came in with a bowl of soup, and soon they were at the table eating. The baby sat in his chair cooing and pouring orange juice on his head. Haliru fussed over him, putting little pieces of mashed food into his mouth, while Labara kept wiping off the mess he made of it. There was a sad look in Halima's eyes as she looked at the baby in this peaceful domestic atmosphere. She could have had a happy home like this, she thought ruefully, with Bala and their baby. A wave of sadness washed over her and she shivered. Some weeks later, Mrs Kadizu arrived to look after her daughter.

Six months sped by and soon Halima was

back in Jos, and straight into a whirlwind of political activities. It was as if she had never been away for she had had regular visits from members in Danso who acquainted her with the goings on. She had not realised how appreciated she was in the Party until the evening she turned up for the usual action committee meeting to find that she was the guest of honour at a welcome back party. Later, at a meeting with the state chairman and members of the executive, she was told that they had decided to appoint a Public Relations Officer to liaise the Party more with the public. After much scrutiny she had been the obvious choice because of her good educational background and dedication to the Party — that was if she would accept the salary the Party could afford to pay. The offer had not come as a surprise to her, and it was not true that she had been the obvious choice. While she was away the post had been offered first to Miss Salawu and then to Malam Ladan who had both turned it down for one reason or the other. The choice had then fallen on her. She suspected the others had refused because of the poor remuneration.

Could she do that too? She needed money as much as the next person, particularly now that she had added responsibilities, but could she afford to displease the state's executive? The other two could afford to, for although they were very active members, they were not working for a career in politics. Then there was the welcome back party which was obviously meant to sweeten her up. It was a tricky situation. We shall now know which comes first with Miss Kadizu — devotion to the SRP or love for a comfortable life," said Mr Ardo, the chairman, with a twinkle in his eye. Oh, the blackmailer!

A difficult decision for a young woman to make, observed Hajia Maryam, the first vice chairman. It's not fair on her unless we can increase the salary or provide her with accommodation to make the offer more attractive. Halima was aware that the remuneration must be poor, yet she knew that she needed the backing of these people to get nominated to stand for elections as an SRP candidate in one of the constituencies. She had not made this known officially but it was no secret among members.

Could she live on the salary offered? She would be fine if only she had some savings she could use to help, or if she could accept a weekend job. She knew she could not, for a fulltime job as a PRO for a political party would be almost a twenty four hours a day job, and she would want to discharge her duties efficiently. She had also promised her family that she would spend every weekend in Danso so as to have sufficient rest. How broadminded were these people? Would they still give her their support if she turned down the job?

She stood up to speak. Madam, sirs, first of all, I would like to say how flattered and highly honoured I am that I was thought dedicated enough to our dear Party to be considered for such an important and sensitive position. I thank you all. I know how financially stretched we are and I'm willing, like most members, to make sacrifices to ensure the smooth running of affairs and ensure our victory in the next elections. But, as we are all aware, these are difficult economic times and there's precious little one can do without money, so my accepting the job depends on the salary. If it is something I can manage on, I'll not hesitate to accept even if it means living on the breadline.

She sat down quite pleased with her little speech. She was fast acquiring the flowery manner of expression of politicians. The ball was in their court now. She waited. The others nodded their heads in approval of the girl's polite and diplomatic attitude. Fair enough, said Mr Ardo. What's the salary? he asked Mr Bentu, the state secretary. Four hundred naira a month, he replied, consulting a sheet of paper in front of him. Halima could not resist a silent giggle. Boy! That was even lower than whatever the notion of breadline was considered to be in an expensive city like Jos. How could she pay the rent, feed and clothe herself out of that? She was not a spendthrift, but she had never had to scrimp. Her parents and Bala had seen to that. Even her part time job fetched more than that. Could she refuse? She opened her mouth to say something, not quite knowing what.

Someone else spoke.

What about fringe benefits? asked Hajia

Maryam. Halima could have kissed the woman. She looked at her gratefully. The chairman and the secretary looked at each other and scratched their heads. Obviously there were no fringe benefits, or they had not thought of them. Mr Ardo cleared his throat, slightly embarrassed.

Er . . . er . . . fringe benefits? he asked, trying to stall. Yes, fringe benefits, said Hajia Maryam. You know, accommodation, transport or car loan, insurance or pension scheme. Well, said Mr Ardo at length, sitting back in his chair. There are vehicles for official use, that is, if you can find one that's in good working condition. I'm afraid we cannot grant a car loan or stand guarantor for one from the bank. As for accommodation er . . . er . . . He turned again to Mr Bentu.

She could live in one of the flats here at headquarters. Oh, no, no, burst out Halima. I'd rather stay where I am at the moment. I like it very much. She was not that attached to the place but she had long decided that she would never put herself in a position where she could be deprived of a roof over her head at random. That was why she had paid her landlord two years rent in advance and she would continue doing that until she had a house or flat of her own. Besides, she would hate to live on the premises of the SRP where members could keep popping in and disturbing her peace and privacy. As the PRO she would be expected to grin and bear it. She knew she would blow her top and she did not want to risk unpopularity.

Hajia Maryam was up in arms for her again. I don't think it's healthy to expect a young lady like Miss Kadizu to live here on the premises like the married staff do. She needs her privacy. The men smiled and nodded. So what I would suggest is a house allowance of about four hundred naira a month.

Four hundred naira? exclaimed Mr Ardo. I would say two hundred. We have very little funds for this position although we'd do all in our power to ensure that acceptance of the job does not bring untold financial hardship to Miss Kadizu. He was an accountant and he took delight in haggling. Hajia Maryam knew this and that was why she had gone up as high as four hundred naira. What she had in mind was actually three hundred. Two hundred and fifty naira was eventually offered. There was no insurance or pension scheme. Halima did not mind. She would manage. The financial hardship would be temporary and could be borne as she did not need to pay the rent for another year. If she won a seat in the state House of Assembly, her finances would improve. If she did not, she would take a fulltime job and do the PRO duties voluntarily until the following elections. She accepted the position.

When she called at Hajia Maryam's house
some days later to thank her for her support, the
older woman waved away her thanks. We
women must stick together, Halima, she told
her and I like you immensely. I'll do my best to
help you settle comfortably into our Party.
Through you I might be able to realise my life's
ambition of improving the lot of women in our
state and in the country as a whole. I have been
a member of the SRP all my life and was very
active in my youth. These days, age and
responsibilities limit my activities. You should
have seen me in my heyday in shorts and Shirts
carrying placards protesting against the
government of the day! I can't tell you the
number of times I slept in police cells. I was
quite outrageous and shocked. My parents did
not know what to do with me.

It was a wonder that I got married and
raised a family. She laughed with self

satisfaction. Halima looked at her with renewed admiration. I would have liked to know you then, Hajia.

Do you want to stand for election, Halima?

Yes, madam, admitted Halima. ,, hope you don't think I'm too ambitious or young? No, I don't think you're too ambitious or young for a seat in the state House of Assembly, but it is going to be a difficult task getting you nominated to stand in a constituency. Oh, was all Halima could say. She had thought that hard work, loyalty and dedication to the Party was all that was required.

Hajia Maryam looked at her sympathetically. You look disappointed and I can guess why. You work hard for the SRP, you left a lucrative job so as to give more service to the Party, so you expect your nomination to be automatic. You did not think of the odds against you. What are these please, madam?

One, you're a woman. Halima raised her eyebrows. Oh, yes. Even in our Party where we pledge equal opportunity for the sexes, members would hesitate to put up a female candidate, particularly when the rival parties are putting up a male candidate. Don't forget that in our country men are the decision makers everywhere. It is important to put up candidates that would be acceptable to a constituency, and rather unfortunately a large number of people think that a female member of the House would be able to champion their cause and draw the government's attention to their area. It is an erroneous belief, but there it is.

Halima was beginning to understand how difficult things were likely to be.

The local branch decides who will stand,

but the State Executive has an important advisory role to play. Your brother's position as the General Manager at the Agricultural Farm is an added advantage as he is well known to the farmers in the area who form the majority of the inhabitants. A hint dropped here and there that his sister is standing as SRP candidate for the area will help. After all, he buys most of their stuff. She laughed at the shocked expression on Halima's face. Blackmail, you must be thinking.

Halima nodded, wondering if Haliru would or should do such a thing since as a civil servant he was not supposed to be involved in partisan politics. Well, he won't be campaigning for you. He'll merely be passing over any information during the course of a conversation. Halima had to laugh. She was learning all the time. In politics, indeed in life, you have to pull out all the stops to your own advantage otherwise you'll remain a nonstarter. In short, be a grabber of opportunity. It saddened her to have to water down her high principles but if she wanted to remain and succeed in politics she would have to have all her wits about her. No honest opportunity that would further her ambition would be allowed to slip by. All hands were on deck to help Halima get acquainted with the people in her constituency.

Her parents came down to Dambita and revived relationships with old friends. Her name became a household one as the news spread among farmers and cattle rearers that Malam Haliru"s sister was going to stand as SRP's candidate for the area.

True to her word, Hajia Maryam lobbied the stalwarts of the local SRP to back Halima. They were hesitant at first but when they heard that their closest rival, the Common People's

Party, was fielding a woman, they became eager. They knew that Halima, whose family was well known and who had become quite popular with the Press, who often referred to her as the glamorous and ebullient SRP mouthpiece, would beat any other female candidate hands down in the area. The ruling Party in the state, the Patriotic Union, posed no threat for although they were putting up the incumbent the constituents were not happy with him. He had performed badly, sleeping his way through the four-year term, with hardly any contribution for him in the House of Assembly, devoting more time to his thriving transport business. His Party put him up again because he contributed huge sums of money to Party funds.

Halima narrowly beat Malam Pam to win the nomination to contest the Dambita seat. Alhaji Suleiman, the other candidate, had withdrawn from the race two days before.

Winning the nomination to stand for election was only a short step towards her goal. She had to make sure that most of her supporters registered for voting. So, she had to include this in her campaign drive as she went from farm to farm, hamlet to hamlet and one marketplace to the other, with her team which included Hajia Maryam and Mr Twup, the SRP local chairman for the Dambita constituency.

Dear Comrades, in the struggle for a better future, she began mounting the rostrum at each gathering, please make sure you register. If you don't register, you cannot vote for me to represent you at the State House of Assembly. And if I don't represent you, I cannot put this area and your needs in the limelight so that you get your share of attention from the government. You've been neglected for too long; no good roads, no adequate water and power supply, not enough schools or hospitals, etc.

She tailored her speeches to suit the audience. If it comprised mainly women she spoke passionately about sex discrimination in all spheres of life, and about most of the laws of the land being made to favour the men. This usually drew a loud applause from her audience, making the few men around uncomfortable. However, she was always careful to end on a conciliatory note saying that the men had not purposely drawn up the constitution to suit themselves, it was the lack of adequate female representation that made it seem so. With the farmers she spoke about facilities for the isolated communities and better outlets and prices for their products. As the elections drew near she grew lean and her voice became hoarse, but she still found time for a regular weekend at Danso with Haliru, Laraba and the children. Her mother came down for a few days each month to fuss over her.

She cherished these weekends for they were periods when she pushed aside all thoughts of her career and savoured a contented family life in the countryside. There were lots of interesting things to do as she gave Laraba, who was expecting another baby, a helping hand in the house. She enjoyed most of all romping in the garden with three year old Musa and eighteen month old Yusuf. She became so attached to them that it was hard to tear herself away some weekends. At such moments she would think wistfully of Bala and what marital life with him might have been. Back at work she would push all romantic thoughts out of her mind and concentrate on her duties.

Chapter 5

Halima had never entertained the notion of having a bodyguard. What for? She did not think she was important enough to need protection from physical attacks, when there were more prominent people simply crying out to be assassinated. And why should a politician, who was supposed to serve the nation, want to shield himself from the people? The idea was ridiculous. It was not as if she was running for the presidency or the governorship.

However, a few months after the nomination exercise, she acquired two bodyguards — Lawrence and Swiza, the latter doubling as her driver. It had all happened swiftly. One day her life was hectic but safe and the next, hell had broken loose and she needed protection.

She had been warned mildly by Hajia Maryam that now that she had been declared the SRP's candidate for the Dambita constituency, she should expect some rough stuff from supporters of the other Parties who would want to intimidate her and if possible prevent her from contesting the elections. Since she was a lady her opponents might not want to do anything drastic, continued Hajia Maryam, but she should not keep late nights or go on long journeys alone.

She heeded the advice although she was not convinced that she was in any real danger. Surely people were sensible enough to realise that if they killed a candidate, the Party would put up another. Yes, a small voice told her, but your supporters would be in disarray and might not want to vote for the new candidate. People may vote for a candidate, a Party or a political policy/You can never be sure which. A little hitch and supporters flock to a rival Party.

However, there was no sign of impending danger as she left her flat one evening in the second hand car she had just bought, to attend a meeting at the Party's headquarters. As she turned out of her isolated close into the major road, a stone shattered one of her windows. She got down to inspect the extent of damage. This was a mistake. Within the twinkling of an eye she was surrounded by fierce and scruffy looking teenage boys. At first, she thought they had come to her aid, but she changed her mind when they began to push her from one spot to the other, tugging lightly at her dress and her hair. One tried to kiss her.

She became frightened and began to fight them off, calling for help at the same time. It was a lonely spot and the few passersby hurried past, pretending to notice nothing. So you're frightened, eh? scoffed one boy, giving her a slap on the face. Yet, you want to contest elections, said another. Let's bow to our future lady President. The others laughed as they crowded round her, tickling her here and there. Time up, cried the lookout man from the end of the lane. A car's coming.

The boys gave her one final push and ran off as the car went past at top speed. Everywhere was still and peaceful once more. The attack had not lasted more than three or four minutes but it left Halima badly shaken. The actual physical attack had been negligible. What had frightened her most of all was the thought of rape, for just before the boys were warned by their comrade, one of them had suggested that they took her into the nearby bush.

She was furious with herself for not putting up more self defence. There were weapons all around her although she had not seen them at the time. She could have used her high heeled shoes to inflict some injuries on the boys; she could have used the pair of scissors in her bag; or a biro; or her long nails; or the big stick lying nearby. The list was long. She might even have used her teeth. Oh, anything would have been done to leave a mark on one or several of them.

However she decided against going back home. She must be brave and not allow a handful of irresponsible boys to intimidate her. She would have to carry a weapon around in her car and handbag and never stop in a lonely place no matter what happened. She cleared the pieces of broken glass from the car seats, and after some deep breathing, she felt calm enough to drive off.

Members were most sympathetic when they were told of the incident and someone suggested she stayed in one of the flats at the secretariat for a while. Her attackers who might or might not have been sent by political rivals, could strike again. She did not want to live at the secretariat but she agreed with Hajia Maryam's suggestion that Jibril, her steward, should accompany her whenever she had an evening engagement.

A blaze of publicity followed her ordeal. A local paper had somehow got wind of the incident that night and the next morning came up with SRP's female candidate attacked and left half dead, splashed on its back page. The rest of that day, other newspapers besieged the headquarters seeking an interview with her. She wanted to oblige so she could dismiss the incident lightly, but her Party's state chairman and secretary would not allow her to see anyone, and the following day she was whisked off secretly to Danso to spend a quiet week. She was warned not to grant interviews to the Press and to sit back, relax and follow the aftermath in the dailies.

For the next two or three days Mr Gwam and Mr Bentu spent most of their time at the secretariat, receiving sympathisers and giving Press Conferences. According to newspaper reports, Halima had been ambushed by about fifty fierce looking youths who had smashed her car windows and attacked her with sticks and knives. She was later left for dead on the road where she was picked up by a motorist who rushed her to a private hospital where she was gradually responding to treatment.

One paper said she had a fracture or two and subtly accused a certain political Party as being behind the attack. This Party promptly refuted the allegation, saying they did not regard Miss Kadizu as enough of a threat to them to warrant a physical attack on her.

Several national papers took up the story and said it was the huge unemployment and discontent in the country which led to fifty youths attacking a helpless and unarmed lady. Political thuggery was condemned in no uncertain terms.

The incident got such nationwide publicity that an old schoolmate who had no idea she was in politics wrote through her Party's national secretariat to sympathise. Alarmed by what they had read in the papers, her parents, Rahila and family, Mr Twup and his family, all visited her in Danso to assure themselves that she was still alive. She was overwhelmed by all this show of affection and concern, but felt the SRP had played up the whole thing out of proportion. The aim, of course, as she realised later, was to win the public's sympathy thereby earning some more votes for her. It was a good political manoeuvre, even though the exaggeration of the incident made her feel uncomfortable. Sometimes she wondered if the attack had been stage managed by her Party.

She spent her idle week in Danso mostly in the company of the children. Musa, who understood that his aunt had been attacked by some wicked boys, but had been able to defend herself and escape unhurt, regarded her as a heroine. Little Yusuf tagged after her on his sturdy legs, anxious not to let her out of his sight, as if subconsciously he realised how close he had come to losing her. While she was around, he allowed no one else to feed him or change his nappies, and he would go to sleep at night holding on fast to her finger. He, more than anyone else, made her feel really loved and wanted.

Halima was making for the car park on her first day back at work when she was stopped by a tall, hefty looking man dressed in denim slacks and a John Lennon — 'Give Peace A Chance' T-shirt. She had noticed him around that morning and had assumed he was a visiting member. They usually had members in transit who sought accommodation in the flats at the secretariat. Such people were usually brought to her office to be introduced, so she could help sort out whatever problems they might have. No one had brought the man in question to her and she had forgotten to ask her assistants about him. He was one of those people you could not fail to notice. He stood out with his height and tough, rugged good looks, exuding good health and a life full of action. His slightly crooked nose and the scar on his neck gave him an air of mystery.

Good evening, Miss Kadizu, he greeted pleasantly, towering above her and making her feel like a defenceless dwarf. I've been hoping to have a word with you all day, but no one would allow me near you. I was turned out of your office and told you were terribly busy. Good evening, Mr . . . er . . . Lawrence Yono, but call me Larry. My buddies do.

She laughed at the notion that he considered her one of his buddies. I'm pleased to meet you, Larry. Yes, I've been busy all day although I was not aware that you wanted to see me. What can I do for you? I want a job as . . .

Oh, sorry to cut in, she said hastily. A jobseeker! He was wasting her time. You should see Personnel for that. I thought you were a visiting member and needed some help. She turned to get into her car. Wait a minute. I want a job as your bodyguard. My bodyguard! What for? I mean, I'm not looking for a bodyguard.

You need one, he said, smiling down at her as if at a foolish but lovable child.

Particularly after the terrible attack on you. Oh no, not that again, she groaned inwardly. That attack, yes. But I still don"t need a bodyguard.

He smiled again and moved closer to her. She moved back, very conscious of him. Can you defend yourself? he asked in a soft voice, and in a rapid movement feigned a blow at her. She swung at him with her handbag which had several weights in it for self defence. She missed her target which was his head, as he ducked expertly, but she caught him on the hip, and he winced.

Great, lady, great, he said in a half mocking voice, but not good enough. You still need my services. Are you all right, Malama Kadizu? asked Abu. one of the car park's attendants, hurrying towards them. He looked from one to the other. Oh yes, she's all right. I was just giving her a few lessons in self defence, said Larry smoothly. Is that so,

Malama? He told us you were going to employ him as your bodyguard. He's a Party member from Pankshin. He showed us his identity and membership cards. Abu sounded worried and he looked at Larry doubtfully.

Don't worry, Abu, I'm all right. The man left and she unlocked the door of her car and got in. Goodnight Larry, she said with some triumph in her voice. She had shown him that she was not as stupid as he thought. She liked him but hated his patronising attitude. First thing the next morning, he was shown into her office. He sat down uninvited and crossed his legs. He had exchanged his T-shirt for a light blue short sleeved shirt with the top buttons undone. His presence dominated all else in the room. His gaze swept the office in a bored fashion, but he smiled when it rested on her. She felt uncomfortable beneath that gaze but managed to return his smile.

What can I do for you, Larry? Are you ready to employ me as your bodyguard now? You must have had enough time to think about it. Why are you so anxious that you should be my bodyguard? As a dedicated SEP member, I feel concerned about your safety. That's kind of you. Besides, I"m unemployed. I was made redundant at the tin mine.

You sound too refined and educated to be a miner.

Thanks. I worked as a technician, but I know many miners who are more refined than I am. As for education, it depends on what you have in mind.

Can't you get another job?

No luck. To be honest with you, I want to do something different for a while.

Have you worked as a bodyguard before?

On a few occasions, but not for a salary. Just for the fun it gave me. I was so effective on the last occasion that I was offered a job as one. Regretfully, I had to turn it down because I was still in employment.

You could still contact the man who..

I'd rather work for you.

Why?

Because of my mother.

Your mother? she asked in surprise. What has she got to do with me?

She admires you a lot. She watches the news on television with the hope of seeing you address a rally. She thinks you'll drastically reduce the discrimination against women in the state and this is something she feels strongly about. She used to be a female activist. She wept at the news of your attack. She was sure it was organised by men so that you'd not enlighten other women.

I see. It's flattering to know that there are women who feel I'm capable of championing their cause. Do I get the job?

You could be a plant by our rivals. You might have even been sent to kill me.

He laughed. We're making progress. At least you now agree with me that you do need a bodyguard. I'm genuine. I can supply references. No need for that. The fact is that I have no money. I can"t afford to pay you. You can't? What about the Party? They don't employ bodyguards.

Well, in that case there's no need to pursue this interview.

He got up and held out his hand. So long, Miss Kadizu. I had looked forward to working for you. The thought of your not being able to pay did not cross my mind at all. If I still had a job, I would have done this body guarding for you for free, but as it is, I do need money. I shall have to explain to my mother. Goodbye.

Halima got up, agitated, not wanting him to go. Now that he was not keen on working for her, the employment of a bodyguard suddenly became important to her. Wait a minute, Larry. Perhaps I can manage. Give me a few days to rework my expenses. What would you like as a salary? He named a figure, smiled at her and left.

He not only got employed as a bodyguard, he also insisted that Swiza, a friend of his be employed as a driver so that they could give her adequate protection at all hours. For some inexplicable reasons, she was glad to oblige. The salaries were ridiculously low. She did not even have to bargain. Maryam told her that what they asked for was about a quarter of what they could get elsewhere. This made Halima suspicious. Don't worry, Hajia Maryam advised. Employ them. It's only for a short period. I shall have their identities thoroughly checked out. The next two months are going to be hectic as campaigns wind up. Tempers usually fly high and violence is on the increase.

She was right. Suddenly tension heightened and there was violence at every political rally. Things became so bad that you could only hold a rally after a permit had been issued by the police who would send a team of their men to ensure that there was peace. Even then the situation was often more than they could handle and the usual missiles would fly and there would be many casualties.

Larry and Swiza proved equal to their task, whisking Halima off whenever things became too hot. On several occasions they were waylaid on their way home and the pair would come down, swing their clubs and with a war cry charge at the thugs, dealing out blows right and left. They also had an ample supply of bottles and sharp stones in the car. They did not always come off victorious and unhurt, but they fought so valiantly and became so notorious that the attacks made on them at rallies became fewer.

For convenience, they moved in temporarily with Halima, sharing a room in the domestic quarters. Whenever she was in, Larry spent most of his time in her flat screening visitors, taking telephone calls and generally being useful. He discharged his duties with such efficiency that she sometimes wondered how she had got on before he came on the scene. One thing that made her uncomfortable was his aloofness towards her. She would have welcomed a warmer and more comradely relationship between them. But once she had engaged him for the job, he had discarded his patronising attitude for a respectful boss/employee one and they hardly discussed anything outside his duties. All her efforts to chat about other matters were thwarted as he replied in monosyllables or lapsed into silence.

She once asked him if he was unhappy working for her but he told her that he would have left her employment if he were, because he felt that life was too short for anybody to indulge in something that did not bring him pleasure. Why then was he not as warm and as friendly as he had been when they first met, she had asked him. His answer was that for their working relationship to be successful he had to behave the way he did. This was the only intimate discussion they had, and she had to accept his explanation.

Her heart was always gripped with fear

whenever she watched him in a fight, and this became more and more frequent as the elections drew near. At the first sign of trouble he would rush her to a safe place, ask Swiza to keep an eye on her, and he would go back into the thick of the fight to help other Party members to safety. He had the luck of not getting caught in the police net. In spite of his height he always managed to slip away unnoticed, looking as unruffled as ever while those caught fighting were whisked off to police cells. Halima was proud of him and grew envious when he chatted boisterously and flirted with other lady members. On the last official day of political campaigns, an incident took place which would remain indelible in her mind.

They were on their way back to Dambita after a surprisingly peaceful and highly successful rally in a nearby village. The cars were in a convoy and members were in a joyous mood chanting Party songs and slogans and shouting and waving to passersby. The attack came suddenly and unexpectedly.

First there was the usual throwing of stones by unseen hands. This made the drivers increase their speed so as to get out of the danger zone. Unfortunately this led the first vehicle in the convoy into running headlong into a high pile of old tyres that had been used to block the road at a bend. All the other vehicles crashed into one another as it was impossible for the drivers to check their speed. The still evening air was immediately filled with the wails of the dying and the seriously wounded. Villagers rushed to the scene to help pull people out of the wreckage. It was a sight to break even the stoutest heart as human limbs and flesh littered the road and there was blood everywhere. Women and children wept as they rushed to and fro bringing pots of water and strips of clean cloth.

Fifteen people died on the spot and many were seriously wounded. Halima would never forget the shock she felt when, on struggling out of the shrubs into which she had been thrown, she discovered the inert figure of Larry slumped in the front seat, blood oozing from a cut on his head. Swiza the driver, who was only slightly hurt, was trying to ease him into a comfortable position.

In her agitated state she pushed him aside and tried to administer the kiss of life to Larry. She was trembling violently and could not do it properly. After a minute or two with no success she became hysterical and flung herself over him, shouting his name and willing him to come back to life.

Swiza gently dragged her off and she stumbled blindly down the road sobbing, a pathetic figure covered in blood and scratches. People were too busy with the rescue operation to take any notice of an uninjured hysterical lady. The wailing sirens of the three ambulances from Dambita General Hospital brought her to her usual practical self, and into action. She rushed forward to the first ambulance driver and told him to follow her. He could not as people had crowded round trying to get the injured into the vehicle. It was a mad rush.

She ran quickly to her car and, with the help of Swiza and two villagers, managed to get Larry into the third ambulance. There was no place for her or Swiza to ride along in the vehicle and, as her car had been badly damaged, they had to wait for a lift from a passing motorist. An hour later she got a lift to Dambita General Hospital. The casualty ward was a busy and pathetic scene as nurses and doctors rushed about doing what they could for the crash victims who had been crammed in there. There were not sufficient beds or mats for them and several had been left in the corridor with nobody in attendance. Larry was one of these. It was no one's fault. The hospital was a small one and the staff was fully stretched.

Larry had recovered consciousness but was delirious with fever. Halima quickly assessed the situation and decided that if his life was to be saved he would have to be taken at once to a private hospital where he would get immediate medical attention. She took him to the Lakeside Hospital on the outskirts of the town.

After five days there, while his condition did not deteriorate, it did not improve either and she had to move him to a private hospital in Jos. The bills were high but she did not mind. She told herself that even if she had to go begging for money to meet them, she would, for it was her responsibility to see that he got better. She did not have to go borrowing as Haliru, Hajia Maryam and Mr Twup jointly offered to settle the bills.

A surge of joy flooded through her the day she walked into his hospital room and found him sitting up in bed reading. He had lost a lot of weight in the seven weeks he had spent in hospitals but he was a lot stronger now and was almost like his old self. His eyes lit up on seeing her and he threw his book aside and got up a bit unsteadily. She rushed forward and flung her arms around his neck, laughing and crying. He held her tightly to him. When they drew apart she made him sit up again in his bed and she made a fuss of propping pillows around him to make him comfortable. She sat in a chair nearby and they looked at each other, openly and silently acknowledging the deep affection between them.

She could read something else in his eyes. Something that had been there since the first day they met and which he had been trying to push into the background. He had fallen in love with her. The discovery filled her with happiness and regrets. Happiness because she was quite fond of him and would have liked a closer relationship with him; regrets because her heart was not free to love another man fully. It still belonged to Bala. Besides, Larry would soon leave her employment to return to his old job as a technician somewhere. He had hinted before his accident that he was looking for another job. She had refused to believe that he would one day no longer be there whenever she wanted him and would cease to be part of her life. She knew she was being selfish. The man could not remain her bodyguard forever.

Halima? said Larry in a quiet voice.

Yes, Larry?

You don"t mind if for once I drop
formality and call you by your first name?

No, I don't. We"re comrades, you know.
We belong to the same Party.

Thanks, but it would only be for the
purpose of this discussion. After this it will be
the usual "Miss Kadizu."

All right," she said as she waited for him
to continue.

Halima, you're aware I'm in love with
you? Yes.

I didn't want to be. I shouldn"t be, for it
amounts to a betrayal of trust and confidence,
but I can't help myself. Why would it be a
betrayal of confidence? That's another matter.
The important point is, is there hope of my love
being returned? She looked away, sad. She had
to answer, and do so truthfully.

Unfortunately, no. I'm very fond of you, but there's someone else. Or rather, there was someone very special that I can never get out of my mind. At least, not for the time being. I would not want to play false in my affection for you. I have too much regard and fondness for you to do that. Besides, you would see through it all. You can read me like a book.

I can indeed. Love sharpens the eye. Thanks, Halima, for being so honest with me. I understand your point and I respect you for it. There the conversation ended. A few days later he was discharged from the hospital. When Halima went to settle the bill, she was told that it had been settled already. Larry denied knowing anything about it. Hajia Maryam told her not to worry about who had settled the bill

The important thing was that it had been settled. Haliru said the same thing. She could not help thinking that an air of mystery surrounded Larry, the technician and the bodyguard. The re-election of Mr Oje Ohifemen of the Common man's Party as President came as no surprise as his popularity cut across Party and ethnic lines and most Nigerians wanted him back for a second term. His Party had captured eleven out of the nineteen states in the federation.

The joy of the century was that, for the first time in its history, the SRP had two states to rule — Kwara State and Plateau State. Mr Ritzan defeated the incumbent governor in Plateau, Mr Sado, by a large majority and the SRP had been in a euphoric state since the results were announced. They did not do well in the Senatorial and the Federal House of Assembly elections, capturing only four and ten seats respectively, but still the situation was better than before and their governorship candidates for Anambra, Sokoto and Ogun states were only narrowly defeated by their opponents. There was a lot of hope for the future as the Party gained more and more followers all over the country.

Some anxiety was being entertained, however, about the elections for the Plateau State House of Assembly. The Patriotic Union still had a large following in the state and the SRP did not want a situation in which they did not have enough members in the House to help the Governor rule effectively and implement the Party's programmes. If another Party had a majority in the House, the threat of impeachment would forever dangle over the Governor's head. This had happened once in Kaduna state when the chief executive's Party did not have a majority in the House.

On the eve of the elections into the state's Houses of Assembly, Halima could hardly sleep because of excitement in her hotel room in

Dambita. She had high hopes of winning. Her parents, Haliru and his family were going to vote in Danso which was part of her constituency but she had registered to vote in Dambita.

Larry was back on duty and he and Swiza were with her. She had decided that she would offer him the position of personal secretary after the elections. He might want to stay and work for her and she would certainly hate to lose his services. He had not actually got a technician's job to go back to yet, he had told her some days before. He was still job hunting and Swiza had not given her his notice. Early the next morning they went to the polling station to cast their votes and later they left for Danso to join her family, and begin the agonising wait for the results to trickle in. This would be after six o'clock in the evening when the voting would be over and the counting would have begun. It was the longest day in her life. She wanted a clear cut victory with a large majority and she was convinced she would get it. She wondered if her two opponents would go to court to contest the results. She was sure the Patriotic Union candidate would since he was the incumbent and had always had a large following in the area.

Well, tough luck on him. A taste of failure would do his soul some good. After supper, while the rest of the family sat chatting in the lounge waiting for the results, she lay on her bed listening to the radio. The children too were caught in the excitement. Yusuf, although sleepy, struggled to keep awake. He lay near her drowsily sucking his thumb. Musa was playing on the floor with his toy walkie-talkie. He was telling the 'Elekson Comson' to hurry up with Auntie Halima's results because Mummy was likely to whisk him and Yusuf off to bed any minute. He also announced to his unseen audience his intention to abandon school shortly and go and live with his aunt in the Governor's House in Jos when she was made the State Governor. He was going to be her policeman and would always be with her to defend her from attacks from wicked boys.

The results for Dambita came in shortly after midnight when the State Radio Station was about to shut down for the day, And to round off the night, said the announcer, we will bring you the latest election results. They are for the Dambita constituency where the incumbent, Alhaji Saidu, was returned with a total vote of . .. His closest rival Malama Halima Kadizu scored . .

No, no, no, screamed Halima, jumping up from the bed and rushing into the lounge where the others had been listening to the radio news on the hour. Mrs Kadizu and Laraba had broken into tears simultaneously at the news. Nanny rushed up to the children who had been woken up by Halima's screams and were crying. Only the men remained calm. They listened in silence while Haliru took down the figures. Halima was furious. This is daylight robbery, she screamed. The whole thing was rigged. I won, I won, I won, do you hear? She looked around wildly. Mrs Kadizu and Laraba had dried their tears. They led her to a chair and fussed over her. She tried to get up, but they would not let her.

I'll not take this lying down. I'll challenge the results in the law courts. There was silence in the room. Someone knocked on the door. Haliru went out to open it and shortly returned with Larry and Swiza. They took their seats silently, their expressions sober and mournful. Laraba served drinks. The telephone rang. It was Mr Twup. Halima, my dear! Congratulations! he said. Congratulations! she croaked. I lost. Yes, but by a very narrow margin. Didn"t you take down the figures?

No, I didn't. I think Haliru did. She beckoned to Haliru to give her the paper on which he had recorded the scores of the candidates. You did excellently, my dear, went on Mr Twup. More than we expected. I"m so pleased. Next time …

Next time! she cried. My time is now. I'm not convinced I lost. The results were falsified. I intend to go to court. Easy now, my dear, he soothed. We'll do nothing of the kind. I think the results were fair. We're all very delighted about your performance. After all, you're relatively new in the field and we did not expect the people in the constituency to swing their support so violently and suddenly in our direction. There's this question of their loyalty to Alhaji Saidu. By the way, I should ring him up and congratulate him. That's politics.

Anyway, we're doing fine in many directions. At the moment we are only five seats behind the Patriotic Union and hopefully, we'll catch up and overtake them. So, chin up my girl and congratulations. I must get off the line now as there must be other people trying to reach you. Goodnight. Oh, hello, hold on please. My wife and my daughter would like to congratulate you.

When she put down the telephone her spirits had risen considerably. No, she had not done badly, she thought as she looked at the score sheet. In fact she'd done passably well. Three years before she had been an unknown quantity, now she was a household name in Plateau State. In future she would perhaps even be more well known in the country. She was down but not out. She took a sip from her glass and smiled. There was relief on the faces of those in the room as she told them of Mr

Twup's views on the results. They all agreed with him and there began an excited

discussion about how many more seats the SRP needed in order to have a comfortable majority in the House and what the odds were.

Then there began a series of telephone calls. First, Mr Bentu, then Mr Ardo, Miss Salawu, Mr Pam and other Party members. Even some members from the other Parties rang to tell her she had performed well. Her spirits rose with each call and by the time Hajia Maryam got through to her, she was in such high spirits that she almost believed she had won. It was amazing what people's concern and well wishes could do. After the usual congratulatory words, Hajia Maryam asked Halima what her plans were. Well, she would continue with her job as the Party's PRO but voluntarily and on a part time basis as she would need a fulltime job with more money to meet her financial obligations. She had no intention of withdrawing from the SRP or politics. The struggle would continue.

Hajia Maryam said she was glad to know that the Party was not going to lose such a dedicated member, but couldn"t she continue working for the SRP on a full time basis? I would gladly do that, Auntie, but I need a little more money. To be frank I've been finding it difficult to make ends meet for the past two and a half years. I know. Well, now that we are going to form the government we can afford to increase your salary. How about that? That would be fine, Auntie. I would very much like to continue working for the Party Good girl.

Of course the job would be more taxing. You'll be criticised and taken to pieces by the public and put together only to be taken apart again. Can you cope with such wear and tear? Halima laughed. I think so. The job of a political PRO is certainly not a love affair, but I think I have coped well so far. However, now that we are in government I know that I shall need all my wits about me to deal with members of the Press.

Not only with members of the Press. As a commissioner you'll… As what, Auntie? shouted Halima in disbelief. Hajia Maryam laughed silently and said nothing. Auntie, Auntie, shouted Halima again, are you there? What did you say, please? You"re going to be made a state commissioner. How about that?

What?

A commissioner. Mr Twup and I are having a meeting with Mr Ardo, the national chairman and his two vice chairmen, the governor elect for Plateau State, and a few others to discuss the matter on Monday. Oh, Auntie, words fail me. I just don't know what to say. Say nothing, then. You've worked so hard and have proved yourself to be such a loyal SRP member that you deserve some compensation. That is, if being given the job of a commissioner is regarded as a reward. You'd probably earn more working full time for a company. However, I'm certain that, at your age notwithstanding, you'll discharge your duties with your usual efficiency and dedication. I'm highly flattered, Auntie. I really am. I can't express how happy I feel. I hope there'll be no hitch. Can I tell my family?

Go ahead and tell them, Halima. I assure you there"ll be no hitch as far as the committee accepting your name on the list is concerned.

Oh, thank you.

Goodnight, dear.

Goodnight, Auntie. I hope I can go to sleep.

There were tears of joy from Mrs Kadizu when Halima announced this new development. They all crowded around her, kissing and hugging her until they ran out of congratulatory words, and Laraba and the maid went to make snacks in the kitchen. The rest of the night was spent speculating what portfolio would best suit her. Accept only that of Works, said Haliru humorously, so that you can get ten per cent kickbacks from companies and contractors handling state projects. The family would become rich in no time. Everyone laughed.

Larry cleared his throat. Er..usually women are given the Ministry of Social Welfare and Cooperatives, or Education — something to do with human development. Male discrimination, said Mrs Kadizu, Why not Finance or Works? We have better heads for managing money and also have more sense of responsibility. Hear, hear, said her husband, and then began a mild argument about his wife's claims.

Apart from the children and their nanny, no one woke up before midday. After lunch, Halima called Swiza and Larry aside. I would like to thank you for your loyal services these past few months, she told them. I cannot find the appropriate words to adequately express my gratitude. I know that the contract was scheduled to end at the end of the month, after the elections, but there's no question of that now with the possibility of my being made a commissioner. So, from the beginning of next month, please consider your jobs with me as permanent.

If she expected to see relief on their faces, she was disappointed. A smile played on Larry's lips as he shook his head. Sorry, Miss Kadizu, he said sadly, we shall leave at the end of our contract as was decided originally.

We've enjoyed working for you, but we'll have to move on. Why? she asked, disappointment printed all over her face. You don't need the services of a bodyguard any more. At least not until the elections come round again and you decide to contest.

Yes, but you can work for me in another capacity; as a personal assistant or something. I'll fix you up. Thanks, but I think the fun I've had from body guarding is sufficient for the moment and I'll go back to.. Is it the money? I'll increase your salary, of course. Thanks again. I think there's something else in the offing for me.

I see, she said coldly. What about you, Swiza? I'll leave too. I do need a driver. Do you have to go because Larry's leaving?

No, it isn't that. He can make his own decision, said Larry.

Miss Kadizu, I've got a job lined up for next month in Kaduna, much as I would have liked to continue in your employment.

A salary increase will not change your mind? I'm afraid not. You see, my family's in Kaduna and my wife does not want to move to Jos. Well, thank you gentlemen, she said resignedly. How long have we got together? About eight days, said Larry.

Chapter 6

The SRP had a majority of eight members over the ruling Patriotic Union in the Plateau State House of Assembly. Lobbying began in earnest as party members sought appointments as commissioners, corporation chairman and directors. The national and state executives had a tough time deciding who should have what. There were many party faithfuls who deserved to be compensated for their loyalty, and the proposal by Hajia Maryam and Mr Twup that the albeit loyal and hardworking newcomer, Halima, be made a commissioner raised a lot of controversy. It was felt she was too young for the position and she also lacked experience.

Mr Twup and Hajia Maryam stood firm. They claimed it was important to make her one in order to woo the youth who formed a large majority in the Party and who were eager to have young blood in the government. There were the women too who thought the world of her and had wanted her as their spokeswoman in the House of Assembly. From her good performance at the elections, it was clear that she was much favoured by many and it would be unwise to displease so many people by letting her sink into obscurity.

The Party had its guidelines for executing its programmes, so there would be people at hand to give her advice in the discharge of her duties when the need arose. Reluctantly the others gave in and there immediately began a heated discussion about what portfolio she should be given. Mr Twup and Hajia Maryam did not take part in this. They had won their battle. At the end of an exhausting week, it was decided that Halima be made Commissioner for

Social Welfare and Rural Development.

Mr Twup and his wife drove down the next day to tell her the news. It was received cautiously as it was only a proposal by the governor. There would be jubilation when she had been sworn in as a commissioner. Several events would come before this. First the new governor had to be sworn in. He would then send in the list of his commissioners to the State House of Assembly for confirmation. This list would be scrutinised by the House who would invite the nominees for an interview. Those found suitable would be approved and the others would be disqualified, and the list sent back to the governor. He would then send in substitutes for those who were disqualified.

This shuttling to and fro of the list could continue indefinitely to the frustration of the governor in a situation where his Party did not command a majority in the House. When the list was finally approved the new commissioners would be sworn in. Halima felt that the process was too long and as the day for her interview drew near, she became uneasy and nervous. Would she be rejected? What sort of questions would be asked? She hoped it would be nothing bordering on the personal. She wore Nigerian attire for the occasion and used very little makeup. She did not look as stunning as usual but she did not care. What bothered her more were the butterflies in the pit of her stomach.

The interview was short and, as if determined not to embarrass her because she was female, no personal questions were asked. She left with a feeling of having done her best. A few days later the approved list with her name on it was sent to the governor. This was faithfully reported to her by Hajia Maryam. She felt weighed down with responsibility as she was sworn in as Plateau State Commissioner for Social Welfare and Rural Development. She took the oath solemnly and concentrated on every word. Later that evening she felt proud as she watched the swearing in ceremony on the television. She had arrived although it was only the beginning.

Her parents beamed with pride as they planned the party they were going to give to celebrate her appointment. The list of invitees was endless and the preparations elaborate. Suddenly, she revolted against the whole thing. What was she celebrating? She had worked hard for her Party, but so had many others. And anyway being made a commissioner was not what she had really wanted. She had wanted to be in a position where her ideas could be passed into law, and not where legislators would call her to order on the slightest excuse and ask her to give an account of the performance of her

Ministry. She had no reason to celebrate. She did not want a party. Her parents knew that this was the after effect of the long months of anxiety and worries and so they tried to soothe her. A compromise was reached. A very small get together with only members of the family and a few friends would be organised.

As she was not allowed to help with the preparations for the party, which was taking place that Saturday evening, Halima decided to spend the day in Jos supervising the workmen in her official residence. She was due to move in within the next few days and was excited at the prospect. It was not a very large house but it was situated in a low density area of Jos, at the foot of a small flat hill dotted with trees and wildflowers. The scenery was breathtaking and she hoped she would have time to do a lot of gardening. The inside of the house was pleasant too, for although she had been granted very little in the way of funds for furnishing, she had made sure that the colours blended to her taste. When she got back to Danso in the evening the others were dressing up for the party.

The garden at the back of the house had taken on a festive look with the soft lights and cool blues music drifting from the loudspeakers. It seemed romantic. The tables were gaily set and a temporary bar set up. There was a suya pitch where the men were busy cutting up and seasoning the meat. The house helpers hired for the occasion were busy carrying food to the buffet tables. Halima sighed. It all seemed too elaborate for a cosy family affair. Ah well, she could understand how her parents felt. They had every reason now to be proud of her. All those wasted years were behind her. She offered thanks to Allah for His mercy and guidance. She would make sure she did not let anyone down in her new role. She was confident she would perform well.

After a long, soothing bath she put on one of her favourite silk evening dresses. This one was in lilac and it clung to her seductively. She had had her hair done in Jos, so a set of pearl earrings and choker, matching shoes and handbag, gave an overall dazzling effect. She looked forward to a relaxed and enjoyable evening surrounded by members of her family and friends. She had not realised she had taken so long over her dressing up until Haliru came in to inform her that several guests had fainted from hunger. And, since it would be unethical to dig into the food before the guest of honour arrived, she had better hurry up.

He whistled on seeing her and exclaimed, Gosh, I never realised I had such a beautiful sister. Madam Commissioner, he said bowing with a flourish and giving her his arm, allow me the pleasure of escorting you to the party.

Halima giggled and nudged him. As if on cue, the guests got up and clapped as soon as Halima stepped into the garden, and shortly she was surrounded on all sides and the congratulations flowed. Drinks were served and guests made for the buffet tables, the barbecue pitch, etc. The party was in full swing.

At last Halima had time to go for some food. She was looking longingly at the dishes and wondering whether for once she should forget about her waistline and really indulge herself when someone took the plate from her hand. Please allow me to make the choice, said a familiar deep voice and she turned to face a solemn looking Bala, as handsome as ever in his flowing robes. Time stood still and something clutched at her heart. She began to shiver and then suddenly she stopped. Don't make an ass of yourself, she chided herself instantly. People are looking. The quivering commissioner, ha! ha!. She took a deep breath and became calmer. No need for drama. What are you doing here? she asked him.

I was invited, he answered calmly. The card's in my car. Who sent it?

Your mother. It was accompanied by a note from her. Are you joking? When did you two become so chummy? I'll go and find out what the whole idea is. Fine, he said casually as he put down her plate and moved off.

She stood still watching him mingle with the other guests. No one seemed to have noticed their encounter. People were too busy enjoying themselves. She was surprised to see him chatting with Haliru, Rahila and Usman, and even her father. The ease and familiarity with which they chatted aroused her suspicions. What did they have to talk to him about? Had they been in contact with him these past three years without her knowledge? Impossible! Her dear ones would never betray her that way! There must be an explanation. She sought out her mother.

I saw Bala just now, Mum, she said. Oh yes? said her mother busily. You look lovely, darling. Thanks, Mum. So do you. Who invited Bala to my party? I did. Or rather, the family decided to invite him to share in your success.

Why?

Search your conscience, darling, said her mother. I really must move off. Those plates need refilling. The helpers are a lazy lot! And at ten naira for the night! Enjoy yourself, darling. She hurried off. Halima stood undecided. Bala appeared at her side and took her arm. She let him. He led her through the throng of guests to the buffet table. Now, my love, you must eat. I can't have you passing out on me. I'll make the choice, we'll sit in a corner and I'll feed you. I only hope I'm not out of practice. It's been such a long time. But first things first. Come. Now what? she asked as if in a dream.

He led her to a poorly lit area of the garden. This, he replied as he took her in his arms and they clung together for a passionate kiss. All forgiven now please, my love, he asked in a hushed, penitent voice. She looked at him as tears sprang to her eyes. Bala, you caused me untold humiliation and agony, she told him sadly.

I'm sorry darling. I really am. The agony I caused myself was even greater. To be deprived of your companionship all these years was hell. I cannot find words to express my regrets. Please forgive me. I forgive you, Bala, she said after a while. What else was there to say? She still loved him. Thank you, my love. After the way I behaved I really don't deserve the love and loyalty you've shown. But then, Allah loves me. What about you Halima? Do you still love me as much as before? Of course, Bala. Would you believe me if I told you I didn't?

No, I wouldn't, he said slowly. I don't think we can ever stop loving each other. Later, as the guests left, it seemed only natural when Bala joined members of the Kadizu family at the gate, to bid them goodnight. He had an arm around Halima's waist. They made such a handsome couple. When the rest of the family had retired to bed, they lingered in the garden while the hired helpers cleared up. Bala, Halima whispered suddenly, I've a surprise for you. Come with me, and she led the way to the house. Halfway, she stopped. No, it's rather late. Tomorrow will do. Whatever you say, sweetheart, he said lazily. I'm so drunk with love and happiness that no surprise can hold any excitement for me. This one will.

Is that so? He shrugged and pulled her into his arms. When he called the next morning Halima was bubbling with excitement. Come, she said eagerly, taking his hand and leading him to the nursery where Laraba and the children were sorting out the toys. This, she began, pointing, but before she could say another word, Yusuf, on catching sight of Bala, abandoned his toys and, with a whoop, rushed forward shouting, Daddy, Daddy, excitedly.

Bala scooped him up in his arms and hugged him tightly. Musa gasped and looked fearfully at Laraba who was smiling. Halima was dumbfounded. Daddy? she asked, not comprehending. Daddy? she repeated looking at the others. Yusuf had no time for her as he tugged at Bala's arm. Daddy, Lego, Lego. I didn't forget, old chap. It's in the car. Go, go, the boy cried, pointing towards the door. In a moment, Yusuf. Your mother's saying something. What did you say, Halima?

Halima had sat down in a chair by Laraba. Laraba, what's been going on? Why does Yusuf call Bala "Daddy"? Please, sister Halima, pleaded Laraba, let me call Haliru or Papa or Mama. I'm not qualified to explain the situation.

At that moment Haliru strolled in. Oh, hi, Bala, he greeted, you are early. He tickled Yusuf and rumpled his hair. Pestering your father as usual, aren't you? The boy wriggled excitedly and held on tightly to Bala's neck.

Good morning, Haliru, greeted Bala. Halima's displeased about something. Yusuf and I will just step out for a while.He left the room. Will someone please tell me what's been going on, before I lose my mind? Laraba says she's not qualified to explain the situation. What about you, my dear brother? It was a collective decision. Since at the last minute you decided to keep the pregnancy and have the baby, we decided that Bala should be informed. We, that is, Dad and Mum more especially, felt you must still feel something for the man to want to keep his baby.

You have a point there, but shouldn't I have been consulted about your decision? After all, it's my life; my affair. Yes, but we had to think of the baby. You could not keep his father away from him forever. I could have handled the matter my own way. But time was of the essence. We felt it was important that Bala shared in his son's babyhood. He's proved to be a most loving and devoted father and Yusuf adores him. I can see that. Yusuf ignored me when he saw Bala, and it's all thanks to my loving family if in future he pays me no notice at all.

Haliru laughed. He's a boy. Look, Halima,

I'm awfully sorry for the deception. We were aware that you would have wanted to break the news to Bala in your own way and time but we thought it would be a good thing if the boy benefited from the love of both his father and mother right from the onset. Maybe we were wrong, who knows? Forgive us.

Halima thought about all this and agreed in her heart that her family had acted in her best interests. It was crazy, once she had decided to keep the pregnancy, to want to shut Bala out of it all. It did not matter if they were not married. It was important that he came into the picture. But how on earth was everyone able to participate in the deception successfully? She must have been blind. She thought hard. Each time Yusuf had shown her toys bought by Daddy she naturally assumed that he was referring to Haliru.

You're forgiven Haliru. Laraba too. I

realise now that you all acted out of love and concern for me and Yusuf. Thank you very much. May Allah reward you for your thoughtfulness. But could you explain to me how Bala and Yusuf became so very close to each other and I did not notice a thing? Simple. Bala has been visiting his son steadily every week since he was two months old and you left him to go back to Jos and your job. As long as that? Yes, but he visited on weekdays only, for obvious reasons.

Because that's when I'm in Jos.

That's right. Laraba, please fetch the album.

Yes, she said eagerly, scurrying out of the room, glad that the situation had not turned explosive. She had not agreed to the family decision, but hers had been a lone voice. The album was full of pictures of Bala and Yusuf at various stages of his growth. There were some of him and his sisters too. So, Bala had even brought down his daughters to meet their brother! That was like him. He would want everyone to know about his son. His house would be full of his pictures and he would have one on his desk in his office and carry one in his purse.

Suddenly her feeling of being betrayed gave way to that of pride and love. She was lucky in Bala, in Yusuf, in her family and in her career. She felt on top of the world. She shut the album and got up. I'll go and look for Bala and Yusuf. At the door she turned.

Do tell me. How were the children able to keep the secret? Musa came forward from where he had been hiding. It's the secret police, Auntie.

Secret police? What are you talking about,

Musa? I'm a member of the secret police, he announced proudly. You see, Halima, explained Haliru, winking at her, everybody in this house is a member of the Danso secret police. To get promoted you must not say anything about Yusuf's real father, who's also a member. Auntie Halima, most of all, must not be told, or else she would never get elected as governor of the state and, if she isn't, Musa will never get a chance to become the governor's special police guard.

Oho! laughed Halima, hugging her nephew. Poor you! It must have been quite a struggle for you to keep secrets from Auntie. Have you been a good constable? Yes, Auntie. I never told you of Uncle Bala's visits and his gifts to Yusuf and me, did I? No, you didn't. Good boy." She kissed him. Daddy, do I get promoted? Of course. What was your rank the last time? 'Corporal.

Fine, you're promoted to sergeant. Mummy will add another stripe to your uniform. Gee, thanks, Daddy. I must go and tell Uncle Bala and Yusuf." With that he ran off. Mr Kadizu invited Bala to the family meeting he convened some days after the party. The purpose, he said, was to explain why the family had risked the wrath of their daughter by disobeying her wish that the birth of Yusuf be concealed from his father. The explanation was mainly for the benefit of Halima who must be feeling very disappointed by her family's seeming lack of loyalty.

My daughter, he said, turning to her. Your mother and I are mainly the guilty ones, and although we are your parents, we're not too proud to apologise and ask for your forgiveness in this matter. At this point, Halima knelt in front of him and said that an elder does not ask for forgiveness from a younger person. More especially if the older person is a parent. Her father nodded and gently raised her to her feet. Thank you Halima. On this occasion it is necessary, but we do not regret our action. We were delighted at your decision not to have an abortion. We were proud, too, because it showed that your moral values and sense of responsibility were stronger than the fear of being looked down upon in the society as an unmarried mother.

We did not argue with you when you said that Yusuf's birth was to be kept a secret from Bala, who had treated the family in a humiliating manner. Later, we decided to bring him into the affair. We did not feel that it was right to keep him in the dark about the birth of his son. He was very grateful for our decision and he sent several delegations of his friends and relatives to apologise for the wrong he had done to us. We forgave him because of Yusuf who had become a link between us. We told him that our action had nothing to do with the relationship between the two of you. We made him promise not to contact you on the matter for any reason.

We wanted you to find your feet and did not want your career disturbed. We knew that you would contact him when you felt the time was right, and inform him of the existence of his son. I'm glad he kept his promise and kept away from you. The family, while not hankering after a reconciliation between the two of you, felt that, as the father of your child, he should be given an opportunity to congratulate you on your appointment, hence he was invited to your party.

You are both adults and should be able to contain the outcome of your meeting again. Yesterday, Bala sent a delegation to me, formally asking for the hand of my daughter in marriage, he announced it to the others in the room.

Halima's eyes widened in surprise. But, Dad, he can't do that. He has not asked me to marry him yet. It's wrong of him to assume that I would want to marry him. In that case, said Mr Kadizu, looking from one to the other in amusement, we'll drop the matter.

Oh no, sir, said Bala, jumping to his feet. I'll rectify the omission at once. Halima, darling, he said standing in front of her, love of my life, will you marry . .

Sshush, spare our blushes please, protested Haliru, Shouldn't this be done in private? The others laughed. Bala let Halima out of the room. A minute later they returned. Madam, Sir, he said bowing to Mr and Mrs Kadizu. Your daughter has done me the honour of accepting my offer of marriage. We know, said Haliru, there's lipstick on your lips to prove it. More laughter as Bala wiped his lips.

Thank you, Haliru, he said. Sir, Madam, he said, bowing again. I'm aware, of course, that Halima's acceptance is only the first hurdle in the matter, and perhaps the easiest. Your approval, sir, is extremely vital. Without your consent and blessings our union can never be totally blissful. Clever chap, called out Haliru. Go on, sweeten us up. You'll be chucked out in a minute.

Bala smiled and continued. I know that the question of Halima's political career would be uppermost in your mind, sir — what might become of it when we are married. I promise before everyone present here that I"ll not stand in her way at all, whatever the political position she would like to hold. I've given it all careful thought, and to drive my decision home, I'm moving my office from Kaduna to Jos so that we could be together and build up a home for Yusuf and the other children we'll have. You've not been given Halima yet, countered Haliru, so don"t talk of breeding children.

Thanks again, Haliru. Perhaps it is a bit early to mention that. What I wanted to emphasise was that I'm prepared to do all in my power to enhance Halima's political career. She's given up a lot for me in the past and I feel very much indebted to her. I hope, Sir, that you"ll view my proposal with a kind eye. He sat down. Thank you, Bala, said Mr Kadizu. We'll give our reply to the members of your family when they call again.

Some weeks later, Halima and Bala became very busy as they prepared to move into their new house. They had gone through three forms of wedding — traditional, registry and Islamic. For official purposes she retained her maiden name, and, after much persuasion from

Bala, agreed that they should live in one of his houses in Jos instead of the official residence provided for her by the government. She was quite confident that there was no way in which Bala could depossess her of anything as he had before. She was somebody in her own right now. And, as her father had pointed out, his action had been a blessing, for it had prompted her into making something of her life.

Hajia Maryam gave a small informal party for the new Commissioners at the SRP headquarters. Halima choked on her drink when Mr Ardo introduced Bala to them as the anonymous businessman who had supplied the bulk of the money for the Party's campaign in the Dambita constituency.

And now that you're married to our beloved and beautiful comrade, Mr Sumiyar, Mr Ardo addressed Bala, we're assured of your support and good wishes for a long time. Please accept our heartfelt gratitude for your generosity. May Allah replenish your purse a thousand times, and may your marriage be a happy one, blessed with children and all the good things of life. There was prolonged clapping and people went forward to thank Bala and Halima. When Halima was ready to leave for the office one morning, she was surprised that her usual official car and driver were nowhere in sight. Instead, Swiza was at the wheel of one of the two cars that Bala had given her as wedding presents.

Swiza! she exclaimed. What are you doing here? My master, that is, Mr Sumiyar, said I should report back here for duty. Mr Sumiyar? My husband? You don't know him.

He's our employer — Larry's and mine.

Since when?

He sent us to Jos to look after you as soon

as he read about the attack made on you by those hooligans. He instructed Larry that he should find a way of getting us into your employment. We've been working for the Sumiyar family for several years at the tannery in Bauchi. Halima looked towards the house where she had left Bala on the doorstep. He was smiling at her now and blowing her kisses. She returned them and got into the car. What about Larry? she asked Swiza.

He's back to his job as technician at the tannery.

When she asked Bala that night why he had employed bodyguards for her, he looked at her with astonishment. Do you imagine I could be anywhere on this planet and hear of an attack made on you and not do something about it? But we had parted and..

Then you underestimate my love for you,

darling. While there's breath in me, I'll always have your interests at heart whether we're together or not. As I told you on your twenty sixth birthday, I've given my heart to you. Is it forever mine? she teased.

It's forever yours.

www.ingramcontent.com/pod-product-compliance
Lightning Source LLC
Chambersburg PA
CBHW060345310726
48976CB00003B/730